The Quiet Life
of
Marta G. Ziegler

Maggie Reid

CROOKED
CAT

Discover us online:
www.crookedcatpublishing.com

Join us on facebook:
www.facebook.com/crookedcatpublishing

Tweet a photo of yourself holding
this book to **@crookedcatbooks**
and something nice will happen.

This book is dedicated to Michael, Joseph and Daniella.

About the Author

Maggie Reid has written stories since she was a small girl living in the countryside. Every Saturday, her mother and Granny Jenny took her to the local library to choose books before dancing classes.

She attended the prestigious Royal Conservatoire of Scotland in Glasgow, studied Drama and has a post graduate degree in Education from Strathclyde University. Her ambition as a writer is to simply write from the heart.

Acknowledgements

My gratitude always to Michael Stoten.

I wish to thank the wonderful Steph and Laurence Patterson for their belief in Marta Ziegler and her adventures...which will take her around the globe.

The Quiet Life
of
Marta G. Ziegler

Maggie Reid

Prologue

I am Marta G. Ziegler. **Marta** not **Martha**; everyone makes that mistake.

I am a fighter. Trouble is, nobody cares. Mum is too busy and Dad travels the World. He will come home one day soon...I know he will.

I was born deaf which seems to worry Mum more than me. I can think and dream and when the World is not perfect...I use my imagination. I can escape...

My name is Marta Ziegler and I know what I want. I want to get a gold star, and fly to the moon on a clear day when there is no torrential rain. The truth is, I'd trade in the gold star if Dad would come home...

I was born to the sound of Bow Bells, which would be great, if I could hear them! I'm a Londoner, and there is nothing better than wearing my top hat as I gaze out of my window at the Bloomsbury Skyline.

My heart is in London, but one day I will travel the Globe with my imagination. I can feel it...

Chapter One

Marta Z None

The World has no corners. No sharp edges, or so they say.

Let me introduce myself. My name is Marta Ziegler and I like to imagine that I can paint on a big canvas something exciting that is different to life here.

I like to hide in the two concrete tunnels in the commando playground with the zip wire where I live in Clerkenwell. I carry a telescope to paint the pictures, and a bottle of Red Cola in case I get caught red-handed thinking of places far away. Mums and Dads don't like you to think. They like you to keep smiling on a long journey in the Ford Cortina and not attempt to puncture your sister's satsuma space hopper.

I hate school like I hate the black smoke that comes out of the Ford Cortina that steams up all the windows and blackens my nose.

I hate school, and I can tell you why.

There are thirty-five paving stones that lead from the gritty school car park to the school gate, and I can count fast.

On the count of thirty there is a paving stone that looks like a hexagon and I scratched out "M" for Marta on the wet concrete. When you reach thirty-four you are facing the two pillars wrapped in barbed wire that reinforces the fact that I am entering a prison. The barbed wire is jagged and loose, and you can cut your hand if you kick a football too high. I've cut my hands so many times, so I am a bit like a pirate walking the plank. You have to keep steady as you walk and keep your eye on the sea of skipping ropes and mangled crisp packets beneath your feet.

In the mornings I play the pirate game and pretend that school is different to what I see. School is a place where I have never belonged. I don't belong because I can **feel** and I can write words that are not in tune with the teachers' merry dance.

It is obvious I am different. They call me deaf. I don't know what deaf actually is. It is only one word that explains **who** I am, or what I **think**.

Deafness means different. A lousy fat difference that leads to being slumped at the back of the class at a solitary desk with a rickety leg that wobbles and creaks. The desk leg, not mine.

Being at the back of the class feels like being painted with magenta spots, while other children snigger, covering their mouths with tissue so I cannot **hear**.

My teacher, Miss Lacey, would love to talk to me in Sign Language, but it is not in her "remit" – whatever that means. The important list of things to be done for Miss Lacey includes a manicure every Friday. That is unfortunate, because she looks like a reptile with sea green piercing eyes and she rolls her tongue when she is angry. Her skin is flaky, and she spits into the pots of glue.

Miss Lacey is a "pointer" not a "speaker" and points at me on a daily basis. I don't like being pointed at like a nobody - being hidden at the back behind the paint trolleys. My name is Marta Ziegler!

It is **Marta**, not **Martha**, and **Ziegler** with a capital "Z".

I am not Marta…Z none. Z nothing. Z no one.

My name is Marta Ziegler and I am not stupid. I wish someone could **hear** me.

I wish someone would understand deaf should not be **hidden**. Deaf is not **stupid**.

Chapter Two

The Z Club

It is a Wednesday, and I hate Wednesdays. The headmaster could wrap electrodes and spaghetti wires all over me as if I were a spy, and the answer would be the same. I **hate** Wednesdays.

Wednesday afternoon is reading, and unfortunately Miss Lacey has no imagination. She could not imagine marshmallow telescopes used to watch a creamola sky with chocolate drop stars.

Miss Lacey wrote in red pen spilling lines through my story. "Not realistic, Marta."

I don't want to live in Miss Lacey's world. Her armpits smell of Gorgonzola, and she has a "favourite" in the class. Everyone knows it. Her name is Georgia. She cackles at Miss Lacey's jokes. I am glad I am deaf. Then I don't have to pretend Miss Lacey is funny.

I am in the Turquoise Reading Group. There are two of us in the group, and if we were to sit any further back in the class we would be in the gravel playground!

I think Turquoise is a secret code for the children Miss Lacey is confused about. The other Turquoise member is Bobby McGonigal. Bobby is like me – not quite perfect.

Bobby has a scared retina on his left eye, so some words are blurred. So blurred the words look like a flurry of snow. The

Doctors say they can't do anything about helping his eye until he gets older. My Mum said it was caused by toxoplasmosis. I don't know what it means but it sounds like the kind of word used by robbers running through a car park. "Grab the sack of gold coins and the toxoplasmosis!"

Never mind, at least I have made a friend. Bobby is quite funny, and has the ability to talk a little slower so that I can understand by lip reading. The code for Miss Lacey is a right hand gesture of throwing a custard pie in a circular motion. The Turquoise Group can tell good jokes.

Bobby has one ambition, to be a dentist. It is quite strange as he has crooked teeth with a fancy brace that creates a zigzag shape in his mouth. I think Bobby's teeth are fine, but he says dentists have to be a mirror to the World. He says when he has straight teeth he is going to fly a plane over the ocean.

Georgia Deevy and Noella de Coeur, the class bullies with no imagination, call Bobby "just part of the Z Club. Z for zigzag, and Z for Ziegler". Crikey!

I may not be able to **hear** Georgia but I can **see** her waving her arms around like a Swiss watch, and a face like a beetroot. My Mum says she has bad manners. She writes stories about her Dad being a Lawyer. Who cares? This is a playground, not a courtroom.

Georgia can do everything. She is in the Gold Reading Group, and they receive a badge with gold stars and glittering sequins. I think Bobby and I should have gold badges, but I have cloth ears, and he has a dodgy eye, so there is no hope.

Georgia is a baton twirler. She can skip on one leg, eat a candyfloss and hold her nose (all at the same time). Georgia has a display cabinet at home with an array of Faberge eggs in an assortment of colours...magenta, turquoise and taupe. I have a plastic yo-yo, and my Dad is a lorry driver. Never mind, one day Georgia's fancy eggs will crack. She will have golden yolk dripping all over her face.

I feel bad for saying it, but Georgia smashed Bobby's glasses against the barbed wire railings because "he looked sad".

Georgia thinks the Z Club are losers. Georgia may go for fancy holidays in Morocco, but she never smiles. Never.

Chapter Three

The Window to My World

I live in a top floor flat with a "casement" window to the World in my attic room pointing north to a Bloomsbury skyline that turns velvet at dusk. The kitchen has a bowed ceiling with a peeling plaster and thimble paint. Every room in the flat is sky blue apart from my room – they ran out of paint the higher they got!

I have a bright orange room – called "mango" if you live in Knightsbridge. It is always noisy downstairs and our landlord is called Mr Shapiro. I sometimes have to hide behind the door when the rent is late (which it is almost all the time).

Nan gives jars of home made marmalade to Mrs Shapiro and he shrugs his narrow shoulders. His eyes dart around the room as if he can sense and smell a scampering ferret.

I do not think that Mr Shapiro likes me, because he gave me a second hand bear for Christmas. It had ripped stuffing at the back of it, and the satin ribbon around its neck is tea stained.

When you are poor, people give you second hand things that they think you should be grateful for, don't they? I didn't have the heart to throw away the bear. I washed him and mended him. I'm sure he's deaf like me, and that we are kindred spirits.

Mr Shapiro has made the rent higher every year. It's like an obstacle course. Soon they will be too high to jump. I **hope** we don't have to leave. That's what happened in our last flat. Mum was crying and we had to pack quickly. Mum sold everything that was gold in her jewellery box. I gave her my gold signet ring. It is only nine carat but I thought it would surely help.

We didn't get our deposit back because Flick my Ferret chewed up the carpet, Nan tried to sew up the carpet and fix it but the rips were too long and jagged. Dad didn't come home to help us pack. He was busy working – which is good, because one day we will live somewhere that's not got a wet carpet and black patches on the wall paper. When we move again maybe I will get a budgie or even a larger type of parrot like an African Grey or Macaw.

Our kitchen is small and there are hooks on the ceiling where Nan hangs silver spoons that she collects. There is always a smell of spices and particularly Star Anise and cinnamon. Nan makes chutneys for the homeless hostel down the road, and sometimes I get to go and give out sandwiches. But Flick is barred as she ate the boiled eggs faster than we could make them into sandwiches and people scream at her, thinking she's an oversized rat! How can a harmless ferret look like a rat?

I have a heavy brass telescope that is bigger than me and was given me as a present from my Great Auntie Queenie who lives in New York. She sent it with a card.

"Now you can reach for the Moon and the Stars, Marta!"

I can go to New York anytime that I want – it will have to be when Nan wins the National Lottery!

Pinned to my walls are pictures of my heroine Coco Bonheur Chanel. I would like to be like Coco and have my designs all over the World. I have a tailor's dummy that Nan picked up from Camden Help the Aged. It was a wee bit crooked but Nan fixed it, no problem. It looks just like new.

All the neighbours give me their old clothes and I'm not too proud to look in a recycling bin if I spy a tiny piece of velvet with my telescope.

Drains are very good too. You can find lovely cufflinks and buttons near drains.

One day I would like to go to New York and see my clothes on **real people**...big, small, and tall. Flick would be really excited. You see having a ferret as a best friend means that you never need to worry about them being by your side because ferrets are fearless but loyal. They are not moody or revengeful. But they **are** mischievous!

I design and make my own clothes, so if you have an old tablecloth or curtains, do not throw them away. You can turn them into something magical with Imagination, needle and thread and **patience**. I have made things badly, but I have still **tried**.

All the girls at school think that they are something special. They have hoity toity shoes made from real leather. Mine are "faux" leather, which is not as good, so they say. I might be famous one day. The girls have proper school satchels, and I have a tapestry carpetbag with a hole in it, but it was made by lovely Jenny at the magical Bead Stall in Leather Lane.

Jenny made the bag with all my favourite colours, sewing in her famous beadwork of garnets and pearls and amethysts. The fabric colours are of pink, sapphire and midnight blue with an embroidered golden "F" for Flick. This makes sense as Flick jumps into it when she wants a lift!

I am working on a range of skirts and jackets at the moment. One day, I want my own stall at the market to breathe in the air of excitement and coins in your hand.

At school they laugh at what I wear. Georgia and Noella laugh and smirk. They clap their warty hands when they want something. It wouldn't matter if I clapped my hands three hundred and sixty five days a year, I still wouldn't get what I asked for! Well, apart from custard and jam sponge if I'm good.

I do not get holidays wherever I want in The Globe no matter how many times I stamp my feet. Georgia Deevy has been everywhere – Paris, Rome, New York...cruise ships, the

Orient Express. Oh, and don't we know about it! She wrote a journal called "My Life of Privilege and Travel." In other words, she is saying that she is spoiled and she is going to show off with photos of herself scuba diving, walking on water, swimming with dolphins and jabbering with monkeys as she scratches her armpits. It's the monkeys that I feel sorry for. They look unhappy.

Georgia Deevy is not my favourite person. She is a bully, but gets away with it because she gets prizes for everything at school. Why does she get prizes? Her Mum and Dad donate the trophies to the school! My Nan offered to be a bingo caller for a charity night at the school. She was told thanks but the schedule was already full. Rubbish! The Headmaster thought bingo was too downmarket. He has been terrified ever since he hired "After Dinner Vince" as a toastmaster having been told that he was a "learned and debonair raconteur" when he was in fact, "lavatorial".

I wear my top hat everywhere and everyday I feel like a "proper somebody" in it. I was given it for Christmas from Carlotta who was in the Circus for years! It belonged to the Ringmaster. She lives at Number 4 downstairs and she can spin plates, and can speak more languages than you hear clever people speak on a quiz show. The hat was way too big when I was given it aged five years old. I used it to hide in it. In fact I recommend the top hat as the best costume you could ever have…and a great igloo for a ferret!

Carlotta is maybe ninety years old and can still do star jumps. The thing is, and this quite delicate…she has a snake! Yes and not a small, easy to camouflage grass snake but a huge python called (wait for it)…Houdini!

Houdini by name, Houdini by nature. It escapes in search of my best friend Flick. Snakes and ferrets would not go on a picnic together down the road in Regent's Park!

As much as I have a vivid imagination, I could never sit on a tartan tablecloth with Carlotta, Houdini, Nan and Flick. It would be too awful a dream, wouldn't it?

I do not know what age Houdini is, but he is longer than the crochet scarf Nan made for me that's in lemon and lavender. I don't really like Houdini at all. Sometimes it's good to pretend though, isn't it? Especially to spare someone's feelings. Not the snake's!

Carlotta has a poorly chest. She coughs a lot, and I think it's getting worse. She lives on her own so I always say hello. Houdini is in the tank (thankfully). Flick trembles when we walk near Carlotta's. Ferrets sense danger quickly and avoid it.

Carlotta told me once that she joined the Circus because her Mum and Dad were disappointed with her. She struggled to read and write as well as her three brothers and she always wanted to dance. Her brothers laughed at her but Carlotta tried hard by herself with a worn pair of second hand ballet shoes with ribbons. She found these in a jumble sale.

Carlotta used to fill up with tears when she told her story. "I saved up all my ice-cream money for the shoes, and when I told my Dad he called them filthy, flea-ridden things, fit only for the bin. I hid the shoes, and still have them today…"

Not everyone likes people with dreams do they? They torment them and laugh at them…people that want to sing, or draw or paint or act in the theatre. Not everyone sees it like I do. They see it as wasteful.

How lost they are!

Chapter Four

Talent Day

Miss Lacey had decided in her wisdom to make today (Friday) Talent Day.

"Everybody has a talent," she mouthed through snarling teeth. I could read her lips, though I do wish she would wear some lipstick. Miss Reptile with cracked lips is not pretty.

Georgia Deevy obviously had to start the occasion with some sort of "Greek Dance" that she learned on holiday. It was very strange. She wore strings of worry beads strewn around her wrists and ankles. You wouldn't have known they were worry beads but Georgia's Mum printed out photocopies of what worry beads were, with drawings of the dance moves with stick figures.

How ridiculous was that? Mrs Deevy is out of touch. Miss Lacey gave her (Georgia, not her Mum) a triple gold star for diligence. Huh?

I did laugh when Georgia put on a sombrero laden with tropical fruit. Is that Greek? Anyway the grapes and mangoes fell off and squidged on the floor. Georgia slipped on them and travelled a few feet on her bottom. Shameful.

Bobby and I laughed so hard that our sides ached. Miss Lacey picked up the grapes, nibbling on them greedily as she did so.

Next to take the floor was Eddie Lawson. Eddie told jokes

in a stripy navy and white T-shirt, his trousers rolled up. He held a pocket watch that his Grandad gave him and played the spoons. It looked really, really good. He was like a Jack-in-the-box spinning around and tapping the spoons faster and faster. Eddie tried hard, especially with his costume. He had even painted a moustache on his face. He got **one** Silver Star, and got to wipe the board. He wasn't smiling when he got the Silver Star.

I of course don't really have a talent that I can think of, so I decided to use my initiative…and use my Imagination. I had sneaked in my sable ferret Flick (short for Felicity) in my top hat.

Miss Lacey pointed at me (in an exaggerated fashion). Remember, she thinks deaf is stupid. I felt my heart was beating faster, so fast I couldn't breathe. I felt like I was climbing a mountain, but in a swirling heather mist.

I tried to take my time, and remember what Nan had told me. "Aim for the stars, keep your head held high. Never look down…"

Even though Nan had died, I felt her taking my hand and leading me in front of the class. Miss Lacey was filing her nails with an emery board.

In my other cardigan pocket were my "props". I laid out pieces of string, cotton reels, and sparkling drinking straws in a figure-of-eight on the floor.

I could **see** the other children take a gasp. They didn't know what was going to happen next. I did…and I was going to **savour** every moment. I flicked my long hair back from my eyes, took a deep breath and smiled.

Today I was going to be fearless. I might not be talented but Flick was all mine and in this World you sometimes have to rely on other people.

I looked Miss Lacey straight in the eye, and dived straight into a sea of anarchy. I placed Flick on the cotton reel assault course, but she didn't react in her usual way. Her narrow chocolate brown-eyes were wide like saucers, and she darted around the classroom faster than a bat in a racing car in Cannes.

This was fantastic. Bobby stood on his desk and waved in delight. Eddie and the other boys followed suit, and stood on their desks. They were clapping and waving while Flick ran faster, zooming this way and that amongst the maze of old rickety desks and sticky remains of boiled sweets on the floorboards. Georgia was the only child to remain stony-faced in her seat. Poker faced and rigid.

At that moment in amongst the chaos that I could see and smell (a deaf person can always smell fear), Miss Lacey dropped the emery board and shrieked. Shrieking is when your mouth is so wide you could fit a beach ball and a pair of flip-flops in there!

Anyway, Miss Lacey had her arms dangling in the air like a demented peacock, and her black mascara dripping down her cheeks, darting around the desks after a much smarter ferret.

The class were obviously cheering for Flick in this battle of wits, while Georgia and then Noella wept crocodile tears for Miss Lacey's distress! Georgia thinks she is an emotional person. That's why she carries around those worry beads!

As I thought I would wind up the act and calmly place Flick back in my pocket to rapturous applause, disaster struck.

Flick, being a good judge of character, took a quick bite out of Miss Lacey's bony ankle. It must have been a real bite, because Miss Lacey collapsed on the floor and Georgia ran to the office to get the First Aid kit.

There was no blood. Not a drop. However, Miss Lacey wanted **my** blood. Miss Lacey was sent home to recover from emotional distress and hurt feelings. Trouble was I wasn't sorry. It was best thing I ever did wiping the sleekit grin off Miss Lacey's face.

Unsurprisingly, I didn't get a Gold Star. I got detention. I was also told that I had to write an apology letter to Miss

Lacey.

I'm afraid I was defiant. I wasn't doing an apology letter for Miss Lacey. It was the first time I used "deaf" as an excuse. I pretended I couldn't write a letter, they wanted to believe I can't achieve anything so I gave them what they wanted…the only thing I am sorry for is that because of me…Bobby didn't get to show **his** talent, which is a real shame because he really is talented. Bobby can play his Great Gran's accordion. She played for the Queen Mother…well Bobby had the accordion all packaged in its carry case and it stayed there, locked away.

Miss Lacey said to bring it the following Friday, and we would listen in the afternoon. Instead, we watched a video of some crazed bloke pointing at stars and I got to colour in a worksheet. Bobby pretended that he didn't care, but I saw a tear in his bad eye. Sometimes life is **so** unfair.

Chapter Five

Brown Envelope Trouble

Mum got a letter today. Official, and in a brown envelope. It wasn't good news.

Dear Mrs Ziegler,

We feel compelled to write to you as a result of your daughter's disruptive behaviour which led to a valued member of our staff being injured. This is a serious matter. A materious matter.

We did try to telephone you, but the number stated on your contact details have perhaps changed.

We feel that Marta has reached a stage were perhaps we cannot provide the specialised education she requires.

We look forward to hearing from you to discuss the matter further.

Yours sincerely,

Mr J. Mackenzie-Brown B.Ed (Hons)

What kind of name is Mr MacKenzie-Brown? I think it's made up. I think his **real** name is Mr Smith. Dull as dishwater, like his murky brown brogues and briefcase.

He **always** sends my Mum letters because we don't live in a fancy house, and I get free school dinners. When I grow up I'm going to get my Mum a house with a proper garden that we don't have to share. With a gravel drive for a famous car, apple trees and rhododendrons with pink double blossoms. Fancy people always have rhododendrons.

Mum nudges my arm. She wants to talk. I don't want to listen. Mum speaks slowly. She is angry. She tells me I have to tell a white lie. "**One** white lie won't hurt," she says.

It turns out that our phone line has been cut off. Mum can't pay the bill. I have to say to Mr MacKenzie-Brown that Mum is on holiday in Spain.

Mum has not saved enough money to send me to a new school with great teachers who will talk to me and I will switch on like a light bulb and learn. She is still saving, but it will take yonks of time.

Mum doesn't know what to say to Mr MacKenzie-Brown, so she will give me a letter and I will smile sweetly. If necessary, I will get down on my knees and say sorry.

If it helps Mum stop crying, I will grovel nicely. For Mum.

Chapter Six

I Quote Shakespeare

I wrote the letter of apology to Mr MacKenzie-Brown and to Miss Lacey. Double whammy. I put some quotes from Shakespeare in it. I thought it would sound more dramatic. I said it must be sharper than a serpent's tooth for them to have a thankless child. I cried as I imagined them both weeping when they read it. I compared Miss Lacey to a Summer's Day.

The strap came off my school shoes today. The one thing I **have** learned is to sew, so the shoe looks like brand new. I don't like upsetting Mum, but secretly, I would like **new** shoes. These are all scuffed and navy blue. Navy is sensible, but I would really like a scarlet pair of shoes. Georgia has a pair of Italian shoes. They look soft, pretty and polished. Like Dorothy's shoes from the wonderful Wizard of Oz.

I suppose new shoes would cost more than what Mum owes on the telephone bill.

Maybe Dad might buy me a pair in a beautiful mauve shoebox tied in ribbon with a gift tag. 'Marta, I am proud of you' written in fancy calligraphy by a smiling sales lady.

As I think those thoughts, I have to sit alone in the dinner hall. A punishment for my behaviour. Never mind, I might be on my own but I can still dream. My Nan used to say, "Don't be afraid of the day you'll never see…"

I think Nan was the cleverest woman that ever lived. She

21

was a cleaner, but was more beautiful than any princess. See, she believed in me.

I promised Nan I wouldn't be afraid.

So I won't.

Chapter Seven

The Magenta Lobster

"The Magenta Lobster" is an extraordinary place. You can smell it, taste it and breathe in how happy it is.

The swirly magenta sign is neon and so vivid that it lights up the whole row of chocolate box houses in the granite street. This is no ordinary café. It is like a fairground carousel with silver, sparkling baubles hanging from the salmon pink clay lobster. The place is like a thumbprint. It is so small that you cannot see it on a map but it is a chance in a lifetime to step into another world.

The Magenta Lobster is owned by Mrs Viney. She is not only a proprietor and purveyor of fine foods. She has become my true friend and my lifeline. Mrs Fenella Viney knows Sign! She can sign faster than a racehorse running for a Granny Smith!

Mrs Viney has a big personality. She never has a bad day. She is always smiling. Her eyes are like pools of sticky toffee pudding, and her hair is twisted in a bun. It is like a little bread roll balancing on her head.

Fenella is half Irish (I don't know what her other half is). Her dad was a fisherman, and a free spirit. He was a traveller.

"Fish are in my blood," she says.

The café has sea-green walls with her dad's old fishing net cascading from the ceiling. It is beautiful, so fragile. The tables are hand-carved out of fragrant apple wood.

Mrs Viney always gives me a dish of fish pie every Friday for Mum and I to share. She says there is no charge for a friend! It is the most delicious fish pie with fluffy flakes of haddock and buttered potatoes like a blanket of velvet snow.

It is the best pie that I've ever tasted. Beats by miles the bony yellow kedgeree at school. The secret recipe has anchovy essence in it. Just a splash, or you will explode she says!

I don't know what anchovies are, but I trust Mrs Viney. Something to do with anchors I should think. She is a good judge of character. Her uncle Glen was deaf, so she learned Sign from her Dad when they went out on the fishing boats. It is important to find the right words in stormy waters.

On the promenade outside the dangling lobster, there is a turquoise striped canopy. You can buy little tubs of cockles or jellied eels. Georgia Deevy says they are old-fashioned. Mrs Viney says jellied-eels help you with Algebra and put hairs on your chest. Oh, and jellied eels help you to see in the dark. Forget carrots. Jellied eels are magical, and if you have had a bad day then they make you smile and laugh like a cheetah, or is it a hyena?

Georgia Deevy may be "modern" but I've never seen her **laugh**. Ever. Only cackle at misfortunes.

Chapter Eight

Daytime Robbery

Mrs Viney has dropped a bombshell. It is her sixtieth birthday today, and I forgot. How could I?

I have to act quickly. I have a Rainy Day Jar in my bedroom. It's just a jam jar filled with pennies but it is for me to buy a house with trees. Not enough for a **tree house** yet! Treehouses in London are rare….like Dick Whittington and his cat.

I tip the contents of the jam jar out on my writing book. This is my savings for an entire year. I can feel my heart beating…

I can't wait to see what the verdict is. I am sure there are lots of gold pound coins lurking at the bottom. As I scramble in the pennies I feel my heart sink, and my feet come down to earth with a thud.

The treasure trove that is my Rainy Day Jar is full of jellyfish and grit. The total sum is thirty-six pence. What can I buy for thirty-six pence…a newspaper? Thirty-six sour plums?

I want to cry, but I am not going to because crying is not going to help. Not a bit. Besides, I **know** there were some gold pound coins.

I never forget things. I don't want to ask Mum, because I think she may have "borrowed" some money for a packet of cigarettes from the ice-cream van. Well, if I don't have anything for a rainy day let's hope the sun shines brightly.

My mood is changing…I suddenly feel angry with Mum and want to say something. Dad has not been home for weeks, so I think it's best to keep my thoughts quiet. Silence can be best in tricky situations. I jangle the thirty-six pence in my pocket, and think of a plan.

Mum pushes a shopping list under my nose on a piece of scrap paper.

1 loaf of bread.
1 tin of tomato soup.
1 bottle of Red Cola.
1 tin of custard.
1 Birthday Card for Mrs Viney.
1 Swiss Roll for Mrs Viney.

Mum gives me two pounds, not knowing I have already spent the loose change from the **last** shopping trip on ferret mix. Crikey!

I say nothing; I am too tired to sign. My hands ache. My heart aches. I am **tired**.

I run to the local shop. "Benitez' Best Bargains". He sells everything, being a general grocer.

I go into Mr Benitez' shop and a bad feeling washes over me. I want **all** the shopping on the list. Mrs Viney deserves a Swiss Roll all sliced up on a fancy plate!

The bad feeling won't go away. I see Mr Benitez is distracted. On the phone as usual - talk…talk…talk. I seize the opportunity.

Scanning the shelves like a magpie, I act quickly. Using my nimble fingers, I grab the tins of soup and custard and put them in my anorak.

I feel bad, but I keep going. I grab the Swiss Roll last, like the final jewel, and place it in my pocket. I turn my head, and good, Mr Benitez is still chattering.

I remember Nan's words. "Walk with your head held high!" (Though she wouldn't have had this situation in mind). I dare not look at Mr Benitez. I know I am robbing him in front of his eyes but stay calm.

As I walk out of the door, a cold empty feeling like a blanket of frost surrounds me, making me shiver. I am a thief, a hopeless nasty thief taking things for **myself**, for my own gain.

Terrified Mr Benitez will find out, I run holding my anorak tight. As I run my knees feel like a leaden piece of glass. I'm scared they will shatter into tiny pieces. I feel empty, I feel like a reptile just like Miss Lacey. The tears are salty as they fall down my ruddy cheeks.

When I get home, I put the chain on the door in case I have been followed. I place the contents of my sweaty anorak on the kitchen table, and Mum does not notice. Her eyes are transfixed on the Quiz Show on the television. I keep the two pounds in my pocket, and I hope I can do this again. In order to help Mum, I **have** to do it again. I have to practice…lifting, grabbing and taking.

Next time I might try a tin of sardines, or a packet of jelly…or a bar of Mum's favourite dark chocolate that she sprinkles on hot milk. Maybe I have found a talent. I know it's wrong, but with Dad nowhere to be seen, I **have** to help. Maybe stealing could be my talent. I'm going to tell no one, not even Bobby.

Nan said, "Life is full of obstacles, you have to think on your feet."

I wonder what Nan would say to me today. I bow my head and keep quiet. Very quiet. I am not feeling proud today. Yes, I am feeling quiet and very alone…not proud at all.

Chapter Nine

The Glass Mermaid

Mum and I surprised Mrs Viney with a card I made myself. I drew a "red snapper" with felt-tip pen and stuck silver foil on the eyes, so it would sparkle on her mantle-piece.

When Mrs Viney cuts up the jammy Swiss Roll, I felt sick. It felt wrong, what I'd done…but there was no going back. I smiled sweetly and tried to stop my feet from tapping like a woodpecker.

To make matters worse, I had gone to the charity shop and spied a tiny glass mermaid ornament in blown glass. I'd used Mum's two pounds shopping money for that.

Mrs Viney's dad had saltwater in his veins…so it was obvious that a mermaid would be the best present she could ever have. When Mrs Viney opened it she said, "Beau-tiful!"

Mrs Viney and I are kindred spirits.

I've an idea; maybe instead of stealing, Mrs Viney might pay me for gutting fish. I am a quick learner. I really am. I have a photographic memory – well, I borrowed a book in the library about it and it sounds good. It really does. So why not?

Chapter Ten

The Electric Eel

Mrs Viney has told Mum that she is building an extension on the back of The Magenta Lobster. It's going to be a family place with lots of seats and a glitter ball on the ceiling, oh, and maybe some flashing lights. Mrs Viney asked me what to call the new room.

I've had a brilliant idea for a name! "Electric Eel"…I think it sounds quite exciting. I've never seen an electric eel, but Mrs Viney bought me a special book about them for my birthday.

Anyway, the good news is that Mrs Viney has asked Mum to sing every Saturday night. Mum is going to **think** about it. Mum used to sing before I was born…but Nan didn't like it. She used to say, "Elvis was a singer and look what happened to him!"

Nan never really liked Mum singing even as a kid, which was a shame. I know I can't **understand** singing, but Mum looks **happy** when she sways with a microphone. She looks happier than I've ever seen her with Dad.

I once asked Mum, "What **is** singing? What's it really like?"

She grabbed my hands, and pushed them to her heart. "Like a heartbeat."

I hope Mum decides to sing at the Electric Eel. I think it would be good for her to follow her dream. The Electric Eel might not be The London Palladium, but it's a start. I think

Mum could be anyone she wanted to be, if she believed in herself.

I think it's good being deaf, because you don't hear the cruel words. Jealous people are always cruel with what they don't understand.

I am Marta G. Ziegler blank None. I can blank all the bad things away. Why do Mums and Dads, and teachers, only think about gloomy things?

I'm not sure...

Chapter Eleven

Mum Gets a Job at My Enemies'

Mum has decided she does not want to sing in The Electric Eel. She says it's because she is too busy, but I think it's because she is afraid.

Mums won't actually **tell** you that they are frightened but if you watch carefully you can tell. They shuffle about a lot and dust the mantlepiece.

You can always tell Mum is upset when she dusts, or hoovers. If she bakes a cake then something really bad has happened. Mum tries her best, but if Flick the Ferret won't eat a morsel of the fairy cake then you know it must be bad!

I have a trick. I **pretend** to eat a bit of the cake…then stick the rest of it under the cushion of the sofa. You would never know. The only trouble is, you have to remember to go back and collect the cake or it could make a funny smell…nasty!

Anyway to make matters worse…Mum is not going to sing in The Electric Eel because she has got a job in Georgia Deevy's dad's solicitors. That is the worse news I have heard all year.

How could Mum do that to me? Now Georgia will really act like the "King of the Castle" when my poor Mum is typing up her dad's boring letters.

I tried to persuade Mum not to take the job, but she said that it would mean that life would be better for us.

What I want to know is **where** is Dad? It's been thirty-three days since he's been home. I know the exact amount of days, because I made a homemade chart for my bedroom wall. I used a ruler to make the boxes nice and straight. I cross off the days he's not here…and when he comes back, Dad will think it's really good.

Maybe by Christmas Miss Lacey might think I'm good at something and give me a Gold Star. Maybe that's why he not travelled back home.

Maybe he is disappointed in me.

Mum says he is driving lorries in France. I wrote a story about Dad driving in France for Miss Lacey. She wrote in red pen, 'Too repetitive. Try and write about a different subject, something new.'

Huh! Miss Lacey is as repetitive as an escalator going up and down on the tube. I don't read what she writes now. I look out of the window, and imagine I can fly away from school. Bobby and I could be in a hot air balloon…a cascading balloon of vanilla, mint and sky blue. Bobby could play the accordion…and we could fly to France.

We would be able to spot Dad really quickly. We could surprise him…

I bet Miss Lacey has never surprised anyone in her entire life.

I'm not going to get upset today, I'm not.

I think I will take Flick to the river tomorrow and try and find some hidden treasure in the gravel and mud. I don't mean gold coins, I mean different treasure. I once found a broach that glistened in the sunlight. It was oval, and had a little piece missing, broken, but it was beautiful just the same. Someone had thrown it away. It had scallops of dancing diamonds around the edge and I clipped it on my anorak.

I was like a Queen of the Jellyfish as I climbed the craggy rocks. Mum said the brooch was made of cut glass not diamonds, but she was just trying to spoil things.

I've put the brooch in my Rainy Day Jar. One day I will

take it to London to one of those antique shops…I'll show Mum it's not cut glass. I'll buy her a hat with a fancy plume feather, and she will be glad I kept it.

Something might look broken but it might have belonged to a Queen in a far-off island. Somewhere we can't see. Somewhere we can only dream of.

Chapter Twelve

Fish Bones Stick in my Throat

Georgia Deevy has found out that I have been gutting fish. Is this my darkest moment? I think it is. I think there must be a nasty smell on my anorak. Mum didn't want to wash it. It takes too long to dry. I have no way of winning talent day with a badly behaved ferret, and smelling like a tin of sardines.

At least I have one thing that Georgia Deevy hasn't, and that is a **personality**! You can't buy that. Nan used to say that I could brighten her day when I smiled. Obviously, she was my Nan, and that is the kind of thing you want to hear...Nan pressed my hand when she said it, with a glint in her eye. The kind of light that shines when you know someone well, really well.

I wish Nan could come back. I wish she could see me from Heaven. I know it doesn't work like that, but when Nan was here, everything was great. Dad wasn't away all the time, and Mum smiled and didn't hide all the letters that come through (the other) letterbox. I pretend I don't know what they are, but they are bills. I also know what they mean. Mum doesn't want to tell me, but I know there is no money left.

I read in a book about a girl that got some money for having her long hair cut off. I've been thinking about it, and long hair is over-rated. If I got all my hair chopped off, I could give some money to Mum. Then she wouldn't worry...and we could maybe go on holiday. Not anywhere fancy...just somewhere by the sea...where the houses aren't so close together that you can see your reflection in someone else's window. That would be really special.

Chapter Thirteen

Nan, and Why I Can't Forgot, Not Ever!

Deaf doesn't matter most of the time. I don't **look** deaf, and I can never wear pretty clothes if pretty makes a difference. As the rest of my class see my potential as being in the "Z Club" I would rather be clever than pretty. Most definitely.

Nan gave me good advice. "Don't let on you can't hear. Look straight ahead. Concentrate…and watch. Look ahead as if your life depended on it."

She used to say hearing folk **don't** listen, they carry on regardless. In the Hearing World folk never tire of listening to their own voices. She was ahead of her time, you know.

Marta Ziegler has to **listen** with her eyes and **listen** with all her might. I want to do things, be someone important that people want to listen to. If it was life according to Miss Lacey we would be counting crayons according to the rainbow. Does Miss Lacey have no imagination?

I have to work on listening, because the Signing World is sparse…you have to look hard to see it in the grown-up World.

If I don't listen fast I'll be left behind. Everyone in my class will learn new things, and be able to spin the Globe, faster, quicker than me.

You see…I have a problem. If it weren't for me not having ears to hear, Nan would still be alive. It's true…she would still be here today. Honestly, I'm **not** kidding.

When I think back...I was Signing too much and not thinking far enough ahead. Mum was working that night. Nan had wanted to go the Bingo, but she said it was fine...she would give me a money for the ice-cream van if I was really good.

The thing is...I was good when Mum went out. I was, honestly. I went out to the ice-cream van and it is nothing to worry about. Mr Toni knew me...and I never needed to speak. A curly ice cream with raspberry sauce of crimson dripping all over my hands. Mr Toni gave me a little tub for Nan...and I remember running fast before the curly ice cream melted. I am sure I ran as quickly as I could.

You see, when I got inside the house Nan wasn't anywhere to be seen. It was like hide-and-seek except more difficult. With two ice creams it's more of an obstacle, but it is more fun. I think I would be smiling and laughing with ice cream splattered all over my face. Everywhere. I went upstairs first.

That night, the hide-and-seek felt different. Not nice. Strange, different. I felt an icy chill down my spine. It was like the telephone was ringing, and I couldn't hear it.

With every door I opened, my hands felt clammier. Something was not right. I was like a black cat that wouldn't cross the rope bridge...thinking something fearful was at the other side.

My legs felt heavy and I came down the stairs two at a time. Straight ahead...in front of the front door and the letterbox was Nan lying on the carpet. She wasn't moving, not an inch. I think she was dead. I don't really know.

I tried to judge. I couldn't feel her heart beat for sure. I guessed. I stayed beside her, and put the tub of ice cream beside her arms (thinking she might suddenly wake up and feel happy that I'd surprised her).

When Mum came back from work, the ice cream was caked on the carpet, and I hadn't let go of Nan's hand. I wouldn't let go. I don't know what happened. I don't know if she slipped and fell. I don't know if she was frightened when she lay there by herself. You see **I** killed her. If I had not gone for the ice cream she would still be here. I know she would.

I **should** have run for help, knocked on all doors, stamped my feet until my toes bled. I didn't. I was stupid, me, my cloth ears and the ice cream that suddenly tasted nasty.

Mum shook me over and over like a dishcloth when she found Nan. She was angry, and disappointed that I had not thought like a grown-up.

How do you learn to think like that? How?

Nan does not know that I let Mum down. Or maybe she does…if she is watching from Heaven. The last words Nan ever said were, "Courage comes when you let your anger go."

Chapter Fourteen

Funeral

I wasn't allowed to go to Nan's funeral. The "family" that Nan hadn't seen for years said no. A firm **no**…and that I'd get too upset. Of course, I'd get upset. I might be a kid, but I've got a heart. I've got **feelings**.

I have to stay at home and Tracy from across the road will watch television with me. Lucky me. Tracy will probably give me a Vimto and a Bourbon cream, and I will try to look interested.

I have a plan. A really good plan. I will disappear to the toilet after all that Vimto…and make my escape! I'm a fast runner. I will run, and Tracy won't be able to catch me. No way!

I've decided that I am a **leader**, not a **follower**. I **watch** people, and that is how you learn. I am working on that…it's the **quiet** people that have the photographic memories. It is, you know.

I've even got a key to Nan's house. She gave me a key so that I could always run and hide. I've got the key, and Flick is guarding it. I am not giving it back, no way. **Not ever**. I'm keeping the key in case Nan decides to come back. Just in case she wants a cup of tea…

I'm going to watch the funeral from the hedgerow beside the church car park. Nobody will know I'm there. I'll be really quiet…and at least Nan will know I'm there.

I couldn't afford to buy any flowers…that flower shop in the village has big vases with ferns and banana leaves and fancy things. I will have to sell the brooch to buy a bunch of dusky pink roses. Do you think it will matter that I didn't buy any? Will Nan be disappointed?

Nan **never** used to be disappointed with me…at least, she never said it.

Right now, I'm going to imagine Nan's not dead. I'm going to close my eyes and imagine the **biggest** bunch of purple roses flown from Spain. They are wrapped with organza and ribbon that blows in the breeze. I can **see** Nan smiling, holding her bingo card and clapping her hands when I pretend to be a ballerina pointing my toes.

"Nan, if you can hear me…I'm sorry I couldn't bring you back. Watch over me, Nan, watch over me…wherever you are."

Please…

Chapter Fifteen

Gi-Gi Sanchez
(from France)

I think Nan must be watching over me. There is a new girl in our class…and it is all very exciting.

Her name is Gabriella Sanchez (Gi-Gi). The name sounds like the name of an Actor like you see on the Movies. You know the kind of girl that drives a pink Cadillac and has her hair blowing in the wind.

Gi-Gi has a pair of sunglasses with a tortoise shell frame and cubed heels on her shiny shoes. Real cubed heels that make you look tall. Miss Lacey writes "Bonjour" on the board and we have to copy it neatly in our exercise books, being careful not to go over the lines.

The good thing is that Gi-Gi likes the same stories as me, and suggested to Miss Lacey about a Book Club for after school.

Gi-Gi passes notes to me at the back of the class, folded over so Miss Lacey cannot see. If she is feeling daring she will attach the notes on a piece of string and dangle it along like a tarantula, weaving through the desks.

Gi-Gi is very modern and stylish. She doesn't really belong to the Z Club. Bobby's eyes lit up when he saw her. He gave Gi-Gi his spare timetable book. He has never offered it to me! I think Bobby is impressed because she eats **fresh fruit**, you know, cut up from the whole, not out of a tin!

Gi-Gi wears a "French Navy" pinafore, which is darker that what I wear, and her Mum, Nadine, is a milliner. To be honest, I didn't know what a milliner was…I thought it was something to do with puff pastry. Or someone who makes flour in a windmill.

It's something unusual. It's making hats! Gi-Gi wrote on the board that her Mum makes hats with "verve." I think that means that she uses wire and ostrich feathers but I'm not sure. I have volunteered to help her stick sequins on top hats for the School Show. Unfortunately, Georgia's dad is **sponsoring** the School Show and paying for the tea and scones afterwards. Therefore, I think Georgia will be sticking sequins on the hats. No matter, I am going for tea at Gi-Gi's house and I'm going to be on my best behaviour. I might mention that my dad is driving in France. This will immediately mean that we have something in common.

Gi-Gi was herself **different** from the rest of the class so Bobby and I don't stand out so much. This week feels much better. I'm going to buy a pineapple from the Greengrocer and imagine I'm from Paris. I will sit on a park bench, and wave my hand in an artistic fashion while I eat tiny pieces of pineapple from a proper handkerchief (not made of paper), smelling of lavender or pomegranate…like they do on the Television.

I can't wait to go to Gi-Gi's house for tea. I am sure it will be a very grand house next to a field. I wonder what we'll have for tea…Gi-Gi has drawn pictures of her mum making fancy apple tarts with sliced apples all perfectly the same size covered in sweet apricot jam. Baby apple tarts that you can carry about in your pocket. I think that's what fancy, rich people do…carry apple arts in your pocket. You can never be too careful if you're rich. You can get hungry when you are buying diamonds or trying on hats.

Gi-Gi's mum is making a scarlet hat at the moment. I've seen the drawings. I would **love** to wear a scarlet hat. It would be the kind of thing you would wear in London…in a restaurant with heavy cutlery and different spoons and knives for different courses!

I've never actually been to a restaurant like that…but it's always good to **be prepared** in your mind (just in case you get an invitation through the back door letterbox on gold card with beautiful black calligraphy).

Mrs Viney says I talk too much when I'm gutting fish, but I'm so happy. It's the first time anyone from school has invited me for tea. I think Gi-Gi is a kindred spirit. She might speak French and wear really stylish clothes, but…I think despite all that…we are just the same.

Gi-Gi told me that she used to have a pet monkey in her attic. She lived in Narbonne in France, and maybe **everyone** there has a pet monkey. Gi-Gi said her monkey was called Bertrand and used to like going to the travelling circus. Mrs Viney laughed when I told her that story. Her shoulders moved up and down like a roller-coaster.

Mrs Viney thinks Gi-Gi has an Imagination just like mine. Good! I think having an Imagination is the most important thing of all. You can climb ice-clad mountains in bare feet, and you can eat candyfloss in quick sand. You can do anything you want. You can **be** anyone you want to be. She has a book of poems by a man called Blake who she called a "prophet of the Imagination." She took me to Bone Hill to see him – his gravestone that is.

Instead of this navy anorak that smells of kippers, Imagination gives me a beautiful swing coat just like Gi-Gi Sanchez'. It is mauve and charcoal, and of the softest cashmere you have ever felt in your entire life. I **don't** have chocolate drop freckles…and I have a matching beret for my coat. It is tilted on the side of my head to make me look like Coco Bonheur Chanel.

Gi-Gi did tell me lots about Coco Bonheur Chanel who was the most elegant lady in Paris. She was very different, and had her own ideas. She lived a long time and posed for beautiful black and white photographs.

One day I would like to look like Miss Chanel. I wonder if she ever wore a navy anorak…

Chapter Sixteen

Tea with Gi-Gi Sanchez

Wowee…Gi-Gi lives in a mansion! She has no neighbours close by…and big windows. I mean, really big windows with big curtains that go on and on as long as your eye can see.

I'm thinking about the clean air, and the fields round about with no houses! Gi-Gi even has shutters on her windows. The front door is huge (bigger than me) with a brass doorbell and Greek pillars either side of the door. There is no sign of barbed wire and concrete tunnels.

Mum washed my anorak, and braided my hair really neat. I have not brought Flick the Ferret because Mum said that would be "inappropriate". Mrs Viney has given me a whole salmon wrapped in newspaper. She says Mrs Sanchez will think it's their lucky day. I **do** hope so! As I stood waiting for the door to open, my knees were shaking and I felt so wobbly. I think even the salmon knew I was nervous.

Gi-Gi answers the door. She is jumping up and down with an oversized hat on her that swamps her face. It's as if she is covered in a blanket of stars. The glistening stones are Swarovski Crystals. I feel that I should have brought my brooch…it certainly would be fitting for a house like this.

Gi-Gi's mother is very pretty and extremely tall. She takes my anorak from me. The anorak is a bit ripped on the right sleeve and I pray she doesn't notice.

45

Madame Sanchez gives me a big smile when I give her the salmon. I suddenly fret in case she is allergic to fish! This happened to a friend of Bobby McGonigal's. He ate a tuna fish, and his face grew like a beetroot and his neck twisted round and round as if he had swallowed a packet of gobstoppers whole!

I'm not going to worry about allergic things. I'm going to savour this moment. This is probably the best thing that's ever happened to me...I am accepted for being me. I don't have to pretend to be someone else to be Gi-Gi's friend. I feel so happy, I could almost cry.

Madame Sanchez gives me a hand painted card from her bureau in her study (where she designs her hats). The card has my name written on it.

"Marta G Ziegler. Hats are not Frivolous, they are a Joy."

Then, to my surprise, Madame Sanchez gives me a gift. Something all for me wrapped in purple tissue with the curliest ribbon I've ever seen.

Madame Sanchez has made my dream come true.

She has made me a hat!

It is a beret just like Gi-Gi's...because I admired it so much. I am overwhelmed...I won't be able to eat my apple tart.

Secretly, I wish I didn't have to go home...and that I could stay here. I could make hats all day, and never see Miss Lacey ever again.

Chapter Seventeen

Number Four Linty Wynd

I kept a wedge of apple tart from Gi-Gi's house and put it in the fridge. Every time I look at it, I imagine I'm in France waltzing up and down the cobbled street spraying perfume all over my face. I think that's what they do in France…spray perfume.

You see, they don't have creepy crawlies in France. They only have frogs' legs!

I have shown Mum my new beret, and guess what? She doesn't seem very interested. She is too busy with her new job at the Solicitors'. She has to practice typing faster at home using a computer program. She is not fast enough for Georgia's Dad. I thought it couldn't get much worse!

I'm actually looking forward to gutting fish…because I am filling up my Rainy Day Jar. I am saving up all my money for a Swing Coat like Gi-Gi's. Madame Sanchez gets all her clothes from France.

Do you remember that I was talking about white lies? Well…I told a big one yesterday. I lied to Madame Sanchez about where I lived. I said I lived in "Linty Wynd."

It's a really pretty place and has rows of big, whitewashed houses with driveways (and big gardens with pink roses).

The houses are named after the "Singing Linty Bird". They are beautiful singers, you know. They always sing beautifully at

47

dusk and at dawn. Men come with cages to release swarms of Linty birds that fly off into the trees.

My white lie was that I lived in Number Four Linty Wynd. The big pastel green house on the corner. If you stand on two fizzy drinks crates, you can see over the hedge. There is a baby grand piano in the window (though nobody seems to play it). I pass Linty Wynd every day to The Magenta Lobster, and I notice everything.

The trouble is, now that I've thought about it I am worried that Madame Sanchez might pop by my "house" to meet my Mum. Crikey!

I confided in Mrs Viney and she looked at me disapprovingly. So much so that I thought her hair was going to fall out of the bun on her head and turn into cascading scarlet flames that would scorch my hands.

Mrs Viney thought hard and **paused** before she Signed. Then she said words that I didn't truly understand (or maybe did understand, but did not want to accept). Adults always tell you what you don't want to hear!

Mrs Viney sat on the apple wood chair and took my hand and smiled in a thoughtful kind of way. "Be yourself, Marta. True to yourself. **Do not pretend**."

I watched her hands, and felt guilty and angry at the same time. I didn't really know what to feel, so I didn't reply. *Why – why – can – I – not – pretend? Is it so bad? Surely Bill Blakey, or whatever he is called, did just that?*

Mrs Viney shuffled a little, fidgeted with her silver locket. "Marta, one day you will understand. Be yourself."

What a strange thing to say, I am Marta Ziegler...aren't I? I don't need someone else to **tell** me that I am Marta Ziegler, **do I**?

In defiance, I put the beret on my head, and put on some lipstick (even though I am too young).

I decide I don't want to gut fish today. After all, Madame Sanchez and Gi-Gi don't gut fish for pennies. Why **should I**?

I tell Mrs Viney I am tired, and she walks away saying nothing. I have to let her down...but I want to be someone more exciting than being here.

Mrs Viney brings me an envelope (containing my pocket money) and a fish pie, as usual. I suddenly feel knots in my tummy. Not at the sight of the pie!

I feel the way that I did in Mr Benitez' shop. I have treated Mrs Viney poorly, and I don't know what to say. I have forgotten that she has Signed to me in sleet, torrential rain and snow and for no money at all.

I think of Nan, and take off the beret and begin to gut fish.

I may have very little money, but I have friends...and that is the most important thing of all.

Chapter Eighteen

Magazine!

Miss Lacey had decided that the class is not working to its full "potential", whatever that means.

She decided in her infinite wisdom to begin a School Magazine. As a class, we have to choose the title of the magazine and all the features that go into it.

Unbelievably, this sounds fun! What's wrong with Miss Lacey? Maybe Flick the Ferret biting her leg has done something drastic…like giving her an Imagination Virus. Surely not!

Every table has to decide on a **name** for the magazine, and to come up with lots of ideas.

I am now thinking of lots of names for the magazine in my head (and they are whirling around like a tin of toffees).

Here are my ideas:

"Ça va?" (I always Sign that to Gi-Gi every morning).

"Concrete", because there are concrete tunnels, and walls around our school.

Miss Lacey will absolutely **hate** that name, but it will make the rest of the class laugh!

"Flick", this is a short, snappy title after my ferret. It is a good idea…because you flick through a magazine, don't you? Miss Lacey won't be clever enough to work that out. But I live in hope. Also "The Daily Ferret" sounds sophisticated – as in "ferreting" out happenings. A tribute to the never-ending curiosity of the ferret-journalist!

My next and even more brilliant idea is that I will be the photographer. I've never actually taken "proper" photographs before, but I've always wanted to. I've seen photographs taken by those hoity toity folk...the fancy New York photographers with scruffy hair that look at skyscrapers, and close-ups of hot dogs mashed into the pavement, that kind of thing! They have exhibitions usually in black and white.

Deserts, wars with little girls running and mud trenches, that kind of thing. That's how you win a photographic prize. Nan took me to see an exhibition in the library. There was a big board with a man called Sven who took photographs upside down, standing on his head. One of his pictures was of a leek in a vegetable allotment.

I am going to take my first photograph for the magazine in black and white; it will be of Bobby McGonigal playing the accordion. I think that would be good. An action photo.

Then I'm going to take photographs of Madame Sanchez' hat designs. That could be a double spread!

Before I write all the notes for Miss Lacey...I am glad I still have the key for Nan's old house. Nobody is living in it, but I know there are two prize possessions in her attic. There is a very old camera in a black, dusty box with carrying strap (belonging to my Great Great Uncle who travelled to Hong Kong).

I'll take the camera, dust it down...and it will look as good as new, won't it? I am so excited about the school magazine that I cannot sleep at night. This may be my big chance to get a Gold Star...

If you don't believe in yourself...who will?

Chapter Nineteen

Nan's Camera

I have sneaked out of the house while neighbour Tracy is watching yet another quiz show on television! I need to keep looking at my watch, so that she doesn't notice I've gone. The longer I'm out...

It feels a bit odd going to Nan's house when she doesn't live there anymore. The garden looks all forlorn, and the wrought iron gate with the fancy tulip design like *Charles Rennie MacIntosh* is all rusty and squeaks like a church mouse when you open it.

There is still the scent of lavender in the broken pots by the compost heap. I look at the front door with its peeling paint, and think that Nan would be sad if she could see it now.

I put the key in the front door, but it feels awkward. I push it into the rusty lock with all my might. I keep my left hand on the pebbledash wall for one big push – and hey presto! The lock may **look** tired and broken...but it still works! It helps that I'm a strong girl.

I have to be quick before Tracy realises that I've gone. I clamber up the stairs, ignoring the musty smell that's like gummy envelopes. I run as fast as I can. Seeing the attic in sight, I spy the old rickety ladder (with one rung missing). I have to be careful. I steadily climb the ladder, and feel my hands all sweaty.

It's very difficult to see as the light switches aren't working. A real explorer would have brought a torch! Anyway, I keep climbing, and luckily, the broken rung is the second from the bottom.

I carefully reach for the attic hatch, and luck is on my side. It opens easily, surprisingly so. As my arms feel like they are turning to strawberry jelly, I think I can see the camera. It is difficult to tell with the shadows cast by the wee skylight. Mind you, without the skylight I would be blind as well as deaf. Frantically, I look at my watch…I have to act quickly. Nearer. I **just** manage to edge the camera close enough that any shark would be proud of me! I use my right arm (slightly longer than my left) and pull the camera towards me.

I don't have time to look at anything else in the attic, though I am sure there are lots of hidden treasures! The carrying strap on the case is slightly broken, but that doesn't matter. I clutch the camera close and take my time coming down the ladder.

On the final rung, I spot a shiny penny on the swirly carpet. I think that means that Nan would think that I could be a brilliant photographer (if I show patience).

I pick up the penny and hear Nan's voice bright and clear. "Find a penny, pick it up, all day long you'll have good luck."

I put the penny in my pocket and blow an imaginary kiss to Nan.

Time is running out. I close and lock the door behind me, and it is a dry day so I haven't left any muddy footsteps. Mum will never know I've been here…

I then run as if I am running for a Swing Coat that's accidentally dropped into a puddle.

Luck is on my side (it must be the penny)! When I get home, Tracy has fallen asleep and the television is still on. It looks like a programme about gardens.

I run to my room and put the camera in my bag to show Miss Lacey. I think that everybody in the class will **love** my camera. I think that being given a job on the school magazine is an honour, I really do. Everybody will know that even though I sit in the back of the class I've got good ideas. I think that's important.

I don't sleep that night…excited about seeing everyone's faces.

Chapter Twenty

Thief and Liar!

Today has been the day that I've learned that sometimes ideas get forgotten, get trod on, no matter how hard you try. The penny that I found has suddenly lost its magic.

I got up early and brushed my teeth with gusto. A photographer has to have clean teeth!

I ran to school, not even counting the paving stones. I see Gi-Gi Sanchez…and I wave to her. She doesn't wave back. I think that she cannot see me.

Then as I go inside the school gate I realise that Gi-Gi **has** seen me after all and she is skipping with Georgia Deevy and continuing to ignore my wave.

Georgia Deevy has her turned up nose in the air (and is wearing another new pair of shoes that are so shiny with pointed toes).

I smile again at Gi-Gi, but she turns her back. I step back, not knowing what to feel. I am confused, I feel lost, but I **don't** want to cry.

Mr MacKenzie-Brown walks towards me sternly, and I am led in silence to the office. Mum is sitting at his desk, and I don't know why.

Why is this happening? This is my big day where I might get a job on the school magazine. This is a sunny day. Isn't it?

Mum is red faced and dressed smartly. It seems that my

actions have not gone un-noticed. It seems that today is **not** going to be my lucky day after all.

Mr Benitez at the corner shop reported me stealing the Swiss Roll and the other things to my Mum. He'd seen me on his shop TV when he was fast-forwarding his tapes. He had to rewind several times in disbelief to view my thievery.

Mum has told Mr MacKenzie-Brown about me stealing. How could she? She is my **Mum**. Aren't Mums supposed to protect you?

Mum signs for me to slow down. She is disappointed in me, and is worried about my white lies. She says that I am in a lot of trouble. I am not allowed to go to Miss Lacey's class. I have to sit and do my work at a table outside Mr MacKenzie-Brown's office. For all to see. Even my dinner and pudding will be served to me at my desk. Where people can come and view me like a zoo animal. This is **not** the worst!

No participation in the school magazine! I feel like my heart has been ripped out. I feel more alone than ever, and wish Dad was around say some **good** things about his "little wench" like he used to do.

If things could get any worse...Madame Sanchez had visited the school with concerns about who she thought was my Grandpa. She had called at Number Four Linty Wynd looking for kindness and the door was opened by a man of extreme age in a string vest who screamed abuse at her for a "bleep bleep foreigner." And, **no** he wasn't looking to change his electricity supplier. Crikey!

Today I have been uncovered as a thief and a liar. I wish I could run away, disappear, be beamed up!

Georgia Deevy is made the photographer for the school magazine. Her Dad bought her a **new** camera especially for the project. Gi-Gi Sanchez is Editor and Noella de Coeur, bristling with pencils, is Chief Reporter. She says her first article will be about shoplifting.

Poor Bobby McGonigal is in charge of tidying up the

scissors and glue sticks. He has been made a columnist. I am so **happy** for him. Bobby is so funny, and writes great stories. I smile through my tears.

Chapter Twenty-One

A Wowee Saturday!

My anger about the school magazine has fizzled out. "An angry person is a bitter person," according to Mrs Viney. She doesn't get angry about anything…only disappointed.

When she gets disappointed she "addresses" a crab, she says. I hope she is OK. I suppose she raves at it but at least it must be alive in order to listen but even so, I wouldn't like to be the crab, I can tell you! I wait for her to stop at the crabs and **hold forth**, but all must be OK as she has walked past the tank several times today without addressing them.

Anyway, Mrs Viney believes in fate, so I obviously wasn't meant to take photographs for the magazine. Mrs Viney says that there are always windows of opportunity…if you close your eyes, then open them wide. Opportunities are **there**…if you just believe.

Secretly, I didn't **really** believe what Mrs Viney was saying, but I didn't have the heart to tell her.

Well…she was right!

Billy Keenan works on one of the fishing boats and as if by magic is looking for a photographer. He makes most of his money taking people on another boat to sample the views and the sea breeze. His wife Jenny has just had their first baby – Beattie. Mrs Viney gave them a special hand painted pottery plate with a magenta lobster on it. Jenny has suggested that I take some baby photographs!

It is Saturday and I reported for fish duties as per usual. Nonsense, says Mrs Viney! She has "dressed" crabs for a picnic and we are going to Brighton for the day! She had 'phoned Mum on the Friday night after my humiliation and Mum had told me to wear my smart gear for work and bring my camera.

I was concerned for my gear at first but now I have visions of me and Mrs Viney sitting on the pebbled beach with trilby-wearing crabs parading around us. Billy and Jenny live in a fisherman's cottage not so far from The Lanes. The house is called "Maris". We were taught that at school - "Maris of the Sea".

I have always wanted to go inside Maris of the Sea because it looks like the kind of house that you see in a film about the countryside. There are pots of lavender and rosemary on the doorstep, and a horseshoe on the door. Mum and Dad took me to Brighton often when I was a little girl.

It's the kind of place I'm going to buy for Dad (so that he can stay at home all of the time instead of driving lorries). Now Mrs Viney takes my hand as we get on the train. We will be in Brighton in an hour!

Before I meet Jenny for my debut as a professional photographer, I have to **look** the part. I don't have a Swing Coat yet…but I have dressed in a summery dress that is scarlet with a shiny buckle belt. Nan knitted me a cardigan to match the dress so that looks stylish. I have got a pair of sunglasses as well. Photographers always wear sunglasses when they are working (even when it is raining).

I was lucky Mr Toni gave me the sunglasses at the ice-cream van. Somebody had dropped them, and months later they had still not been claimed. They are tortoiseshell and look like Gi-Gi Sanchez' glasses.

I look in the small mirror on the bathroom cabinet, and I look different. I look like a photographer should. I carry a biro pen, and a notebook (just in case). Mum wants me to wear my navy anorak but I have deliberately left it at home.

I have already practised taking action photographs of Flick, and they look really good. The only trouble was…in some of the pictures she has "red eyes" and her feet are a little blurry. She will not stay **still** but you can't always be perfect when you are learning. Mum has the pleasure of Flick for the day. Last time on a train, Flick peered out from under my top hat and yawned. This was enough for several people to reach for the communication cord at once.

Mrs Viney has also come prepared. She is wearing open-toe sandals, and a floral dress. In the picnic are my best things: bridge rolls, buttermilk scones. She made meringues…tiny ones filled with cream and strawberries! I am going to look very professional as I arrive with Mrs Viney carrying the picnic between us – walking down the hill from the London train!

Mrs Viney says that Jenny is a new Mum, and new Mums don't have time to make sandwiches. This way, she says we can make a wish for the new baby.

As we cycle along the gritty path we can smell the salty sea air, and hear the gentle waves lapping. It is a gentle, calming day with not a storm cloud in the sky. I love it here. I feel free.

I am glad I wore my sunglasses because the sun is so golden and warm that I feel I could climb every mountain! As we near Maris, I see Gi-Gi Sanchez playing with a bucket and spade! Madame Sanchez pretends she doesn't see me (even though I know she has).

I show better manners by smiling at Gi-Gi. She smiles back, but Madame Sanchez takes her hand and leads her away from us.

Perhaps I should feel stupid, but I don't. I lied about living at Number Four Linty Wynd to impress Madame Sanchez because she owns lots of pretty things. Lots of expensive, pretty things. And gave me a beret. I will put it through her letterbox before she asks for it back.

I may have told white lies, but I'm still the same person inside. I'm still the same Marta with a broken brooch for treasure, and big dreams. People like Georgia Deevy and Madame Sanchez can try as they might...but they'll never take my dreams away. Not ever.

Today was a lovely day...where I realised who I was. I don't need to wear a red beret to be important. I took photographs of baby Beattie smiling against the backdrop of the aqua waves, and I felt good.

I felt important.

For the first time I seized an opportunity just like Mrs Viney said. It didn't feel silly, it felt good. I may lead a quiet life...but I will start **hoping**.

I really will.

Chapter Twenty-Two

Miss Lacey Leaving

The Friday after Brighton. I have just heard the best news ever. Miss Lacey is leaving her job as our class teacher! Yay!

She drew an aeroplane in pink chalk on the board to give us a clue to where she is going. Even better news...she is going to Australia. Hurray! Poor Miss Lacey has no imagination at all. Her drawing of an aeroplane was very precise. I saw her copy it out of a magazine. She could have drawn a koala bear or something like that, couldn't she? From her head?

Even funnier than her drawing on the board was that Miss Lacey is obviously a very poor judge of Expectations. As a parting gift to everyone in the class she gave us all a small photograph of herself dressed in a khaki explorer's outfit, hat with hanging corks, and waving. She looked very manic, and very stupid.

I am going to use the photograph as a doorstep for our draughty front door. A few muddy footprints are what are required. Yes, I admit, I sound mean...but this has been a very long school year sitting at the back of the class at the "Z Table" behind the watercolour trolleys.

I think it is about time Bobby McGonigal got to play the accordion (that's his big talent) instead of tidying up rolls of sellotape and paintbrushes. I think Bobby has been ignored for too long. I think that having a bad eye is like being the caterpillar not the butterfly. It's like being in a jam jar with the lid on...on a scorching hot day. But he has had an article accepted called "The Lanes of Brighton by Marta G. Ziegler".

Today, on hearing the news that Miss Lacey is leaving, I did a **bad** thing. I **mocked** and laughed at her. Not only that, I **planned** it coldly. I wanted to mock her, but also wanted the other "Z Club" members to have a chance to show how they felt. I thought that they **deserved** it, just like I did.

Everyone, small or tall, should be heard. It's time Georgia Deevy was tidying up glue sticks, and sweeping floors. Having money in your pocket should not mean laughing at others who can only **look** in shop windows. One day Georgia Deevy will know that you have to earn respect. She just dangles from her Dad's coat-belt.

Nan is watching over me...I can feel it. I am proud to be **Marta G.** Ziegler. I am proud to write **what** I want, when I want, if I want, for **whom** I want. These are my diaries and they **will** be read. I will find my **audience** and we will **love** each other and we will have a laugh along the way!

If people don't like me, then they can eat a gumbo or juggle a jellyfish. Being smart or different is **harder** than simply accepting second best.

Anyway, my plan worked like a dream. Miss Lacey wrote "Goodbye and Good Luck" in very big handwriting on the board and I stepped into action, like a warrior. Just like Braveheart played by Craig Daniels.

I clambered up on top of my creaky, rickety old desk...and do you know what I did? I **stood tall**. I stood like a Warrior and held up my photographs of Baby Beattie.

Do you know what I was doing? I was showing that I was good at something! I could be one of those professional photographers, or indeed anything I wanted. Smile, say cheese!

I held my arms up high, balancing on my desk, even though it felt like it was tipping over. I was the Warrior for the rest of the Z Club. Then I held my photographs high (reaching for the ceiling, reaching for the stars). As if by magic, I let the photographs go. They were dancing in mid air. The pictures of Beautiful Baby Beattie were flying high. The pictures were like a flurry of snow…whirling, fluttering in my quiet, silent World. This was the happiest I've even been. I wasn't scared. If I was to be punished, and sent to Mr MacKenzie-Brown's murky office, I was not scared.

As the photographs landed on the floorboards, Miss Lacey stood frozen and stunned. Her eyes were like saucers, and her mouth opened wide. This was fun!

Then the second part of the plan was put into place: I started clapping my hands. Slow clapping – a fake type of applause. I didn't clap for Miss Lacey as a vote of thanks. In my mind I clapped for Bobby McGonigal. I clapped for The Z Club. I clapped for Hilda – who got her free school dinner ticket **last** every day and had to stand waiting red in the face. Hello Hilda! You have been away, hope you are OK today you are with us.

I clapped for myself. It's strange…

Then I felt so happy when Bobby and Hilda stood on their desks at the back of the classroom and clapped. They too wanted to stand **tall**. Wowee!

We were not just children, but individuals with our own thoughts, dreams, and tired of being laughed at. Within minutes…it was like I held the key…and that the class were working together, standing united like clockwork. The only pupils staying seated were Georgia and Noella the Heart.

Mr MacKenzie-Brown quickly arrived because of all the commotion. Miss Lacey sat slumped at her desk. Her head was bowed. She was crying. I think they may have been "crocodile tears", but I am not so sure! Mr Mackenzie-Brown awkwardly gave her a tissue. He looked very uneasy…it was like he was the Sheriff, and we were the Outlaws.

But for this moment, we held the cards!

For over a minute…everyone apart from Georgia stayed

standing. When we eventually sat down, I felt exhausted. Strangely though…I felt a little sorry for Miss Lacey. Did she realise we did not like her? Did she realise that she had showing her favourites too **clearly**? They say you shouldn't have favourites but that's **impossible**. But you **should** control what you **can** control.

I felt a little sorry for her because Mr MacKenzie-Brown had seen her humiliated, and laughed at. Being bullied myself for so long…I had planned revenge. That is a double-edged sword. It doesn't always feel good, or just.

Chapter Twenty-Three

Marshmallows

I found a note in my navy anorak stapled to a little plastic bag of marshmallows. The note was scribbled in pencil, and was only of one word: "Sorry."

It was signed by Gi-Gi Sanchez. I don't know if I'm ready to forgive her. I think she may be a fair weather friend now that she skips with Georgia Deevy and Noella de Coeur. I have to think first before I jump in with two feet with that one.

Maybe I just like Gi-Gi because of her fancy clothes and big house. Maybe...I just like the idea of who **I could be**. Right now, I don't know what to think.

Secretly, I'm relieved I don't live in Linty Wynd. Not only have I escaped the man in the wife-beater (string vest) but also those Dads that wear fancy suits and silk ties and probably worry too much for comfort and the comfort of those around them, and go to Banks a lot. All my money is in my Rainy Day Jar...which is much less of a worry. Nothing much to worry about there.

At this moment in time Miss Lacey will have packed her suitcase and be on an aeroplane – to Australia.

Shall I laugh or cry?

Chapter Twenty-Four

New Teacher – New Start

Monday.

As in a puff of satsuma smoke, Miss Lacey was gone and her desk cleared of the array of bad taste nail varnish and emery boards.

If our class was like a space ship then there was a new pilot at the helm. I had a sleepless night, tossing and turning…and thinking. I imagined that I might get a job on the school magazine at last. My slate wiped clean by a new teacher.

Mrs Viney was very stern in her Signing yesterday. She told me that a new teacher was a new beginning. I had to give the new teacher a chance. I had to stop looking backwards. I can do that! Mrs Viney says that I am "too black and white" a person. What does that mean?

I have been imagining what our new teacher will be like. Hopefully she will be a lady with a Swing Coat, cubed heels, chunky beads and nice hair. Someone who reads lots of books (with funny pictures). Oh, and someone who is fun, fun, fun!

Someone who smiles, and doesn't look like a reptile Also someone without dandruff flake issues.

Chapter Twenty-Five

Topsy Turvy!

Who **is** going to be the new pilot of "The Space Ship Z"?

I run down the uneven pavement to school, and I am careful about tripping on the last paving stone that juts out like a magical crystal. I do not want a bruised knee and ripped stockings on my first day with the new teacher. I have even brushed my hair today so there are no tangles in it.

As we form an orderly line to go into the classroom...my heart is beating fast...and my hands feel tingly. Mrs Viney says that I fidget too much and I don't concentrate on what I'm doing. I suppose I'm fidgeting a little now. I brought my broken brooch for luck and company.

It is too soon to introduce the new teacher to Flick the Ferret. They could be allergic, or a vegetarian, you never know, do you? Anyway, the new teacher has blacked out the windows and door with black card. None of us can see in. It looks a little spooky, but fun at the same time. A mixture.

When we eventually get into our classroom...it is unrecognisable. It is transformed. It is like Miss Lacey never existed.

There are no tables at the back of the classroom. There are new desks instead of the old, scraped wooden ones (with writing etched on them that are never in straight lines and filled in with black ink from Dickens' time). The desks are sky blue, and circular, with brightly coloured chairs in red, bright sunny yellow, and green.

The tables are spaced out (so you can walk around them). It feels like you can **breathe** in the classroom. It is now not all tense and crammed and claustrophobic at all. This feels like a new beginning ,just like Mrs Viney said.

Unfortunately…I spoke too soon. Far too soon!

When I first saw **him**, I could not believe it. He did not look like the suitable candidate for a Space-Ship Pilot. You would expect a male pilot to have a razor sharp nose, be tall and carry a manual about planets – the Moon, the Stars and things like that.

A male pilot should be strong…like an athlete. Unfortunately our new teacher, Mr Gregor Green looks like **none of the above**. On first sight he looks dull and fragile.

Mr Green is small, thin, with bony, long, twig-like fingers. He has spectacles with thick lenses, jet black and lopsided on his weasel-like nose. His hair is thinning and is swept harshly all on one side and held down with shiny grease that he keeps in a bottle on his desk.

His suit is ill fitting and is mushroom coloured, in the kind of linen material that people wear when they travel on Ferries. His trousers swing well high above his tartan socks.

He is wearing a watch that looks old fashioned (maybe it was his Great Great Granddad's). It has a big clock face…and it looks like a Swiss Watch. Every so often he frowns at it and taps it to restart it. Then he asks us for the time. He eats tinned haggis at his desk at lunchtime when the other teachers are at The Slaughtered Lamb pub sighing at the wisdom of the Headmaster as they stand him single malts (sssh…that is what I have heard!).

How do I know his name is Gregor Green so quickly? He has a sticker on his suit with his name on with the Saltire and a sprig of white heather on either side. I think he must be Scottish.

Even though there are new brightly coloured tables...I feel that Mr Green is **not** going to be a kindred spirit. He is not what I expected at all.

Mine is a morning of bitter disappointment! If I had a name like Gregor Green I'd change it...to something like Gabriel Ganzuchinni or something like that (you know names like Actors have, that flow off the tongue). Gabriel Ganzuchinni flows of the tongue...definitely.

Mr Green probably has a navy anorak in his wardrobe, and builds pyramids and towers out of matchsticks (that he counts with precision). He saves used matches in a separate box from unused ones and once put a still glowing one in the wrong box by mistake. It's an amusing anecdote that he tells any one that listens – even signing it to me. He likes it when you smile and shake your head at this joke about how the box exploded in flames.

Just wait till I tell Mrs Viney...

Chapter Twenty-Six

Socrates!

Mr Green has started his new job with gusto! He may not be as bad as I first thought. He can Sign – not quickly, but he tries to learn a new word every day. He teaches by constantly asking questions and picking an answerer without waiting for them to put their hands up. He says everyone knows a million times more than they think they do. The top mind, as he calls it, is only the tip of the iceberg. He has a jade statue of a funny-faced man in a sheet which he has placed between his grease jar and his tins of haggis. He is single for some reason but is happy with his black Bombay Cat, his white budgerigar and his tank of guppies.

I get to sit at the table near the board, and Mr Green. He thinks I should be **included** in activities, not just colouring in pamphlets.

The groups are mixed up now and Georgia Deevy is furious. She has sat on the same table, with her little followers, for years. Georgia fears change, I think.

Mr Green put on the board today "to question and to BE questioned is to LEARN". It sounds very grand, doesn't it? Like the kind of thing you would say on stage. As you know, I Marta Ziegler, always ask and answer so Mr Green might, just **might**, be a kindred spirit after all!

Chapter Twenty-Seven

Invention!

Well, Mr Green is very different from what he first appeared to be. A month with us now and when we arrived in class today he had written a huge word in multi-coloured letters on the board:

"INVENTION".

He seemed very over-excited and animated about the word. The title "INVENTION" is our big project. We get a grade... not by working by ourselves...but as working as part of a team. A Symposium – he wrote this on the board as well, and I copied it into my notebook to use later.

He blacked out the classroom windows with heavy card and masking tape to show off what he bought with some of the funds from the school fete. He has bought stage lights...fancy ones...with coloured bits on that transform the lights into a wash of colour. They are called "gels".

Bobby volunteered to assist Mr Green, learning how to fade out the lights gradually. Bobby was grinning from ear to ear.

He then had to put a spotlight on the middle of the classroom floor. This seemed a bit strange because Mr Green hadn't tidied up the classroom properly. It was a right old mess. There were boxes (old tatty cardboard ones), bricks, pieces of string, potato sacks, egg boxes and black bin bags. Anything that you would throw out with chip papers...was sitting rather forlornly on the pretend stage.

Nobody really understood what was going on. What was the reason for all this? It wasn't like a "proper" lesson.

"Great inventions often arise from ashes. We can create a Phoenix that will rise from the flames…if we just start thinking," said Mr Green.

I think Mr Green has been reading too many of those hoity-toity books that tell you how to teach children in an interesting way. What has a Phoenix and ashes to do with a pile of scraps? Maybe he would produce a lighter, and burn the school down?

Within minutes all was to be revealed…we got a booklet called "My Invention". Everyone has to write **ideas**, and **thoughts** in their Invention Diary. You can choose **any** of the rubbish that Mr Green has chosen, and **transform** it into something magical. Something completely different.

Maybe, just maybe, this could be a lot of fun. I have decided that I am going to use the black bin bags. I'm thinking over my idea.

I'm going to make a ball gown for a Mermaid…and as I gut fish every week…that is my idea. I'm going to use the "Pearls of the Sea". I'm going to create something that a **Mermaid** would love to wear. I know what you're thinking…Mermaids are not **real**. They are pretend, figments of someone's imagination. Well, Mrs Viney has it on good authority that mermaids are real.

Fishermen for centuries have peered over the side of boats and seen the waves change colour from icy, salty grey to a vivid turquoise where the mermaids are swimming. The waves become so bright you have to squint your eyes.

When the mermaids are dancing (invisible to those that won't believe), fishermen catch twice the amount of fish. It's true!

Mrs Viney says that mermaids come to those in peril on the seas.

Mrs Viney has a tailor's dummy…so I can use that to design my gown. I'm going to take my time…and plan. This is brilliant. I can almost feel my brain ticking away like a clockwork toy. I now have the mind of an Inventor.

Just call me Marta Ziegler, Inventor Extraordinaire! I need to start wearing my sunglasses to school. Inventors **always** wear glasses…and carry a rolled up newspaper under their arm (you know a **thick** newspaper with not many photographs and lots of writing). Yes, I am really going to **think** like an Inventor!

Chapter Twenty-Eight

A Letter from Dad

That evening, just as I settle in to thinking like an Inventor, Mum brings me a letter. Mum is acting really odd these days. I don't know if it is the new typing job, or that she doesn't like giving me letters from Dad.

I don't understand Mum. She should be over the Moon that Dad still writes when he is so busy driving lorries…except she is clearly unhappy. Mum looks anxious as she gives me the letter. She is sucking her cheekbones in like a lemon face. She is tense. Mum always sucks her cheekbones in when she is tense.

I tell Mum that I would like to read the letter in private. I might not be an adult but I still want to read the words in peace, without prying eyes. Mum looked a bit sad when I asked her to leave…but being honest is a good quality, isn't it?

I couldn't wait to open the envelope. I love Dad's handwriting. It is neater than mine and all his letters look the same size. I have sprawling handwriting like a plate of spaghetti (at least that's what Miss Lacey said).

Dad writes with **care**. He always used to write slowly. Dad taught me all my letters. Dad was the one that pushed and pushed to find me a teacher that could Sign. Dad (unlike Mum) thinks I'm capable of anything…that's why he wants me to get a scholarship at a **good** school. Dad wishes that he had got a Good Education when he was a boy. Dad wished he'd got "chances."

Dad has taught me that "chances" are what you need to be someone important. Now that I've got Mr Green (a good teacher) I'm going to try harder. I really am. My hands are trembling and my tummy feels light and bubbly. I can't wait to hear when Dad's coming back.

Maybe he will bring me something from the Ferry…like a new pen, or sharpener. Something small, but something that I can keep. I keep **all the things** from the Ferry inside my dressing table drawer. Dad **made** me the dressing table (and he varnished it and everything). It looks **very, very** expensive… and the best thing is that it's made out of the spare wood from Dad making the rabbit, guinea pig and ferret houses.

As I read the letter, I sit down to think.

Dear Marta,

I hope you are being good, and enjoying the sunny weather. I'm sure you and Flick are running circles around Mum as usual!

I don't quite know how to write this letter. I suppose it's the kind of letter you don't plan to write…it's almost accidental. The thing is…I won't be home from France for your birthday. There are lots of deliveries and it's always good to make extra pennies. Mum says that you would like a Swing Coat, so I have sent Mum some money to buy you just what you want. There is also an extra envelope for new shoes. I know you like red leather shoes.

The thing is, Marta, and there is no easy way to say this… I'm struggling. I can't find the words…I'm not coming home again to live with Mum. I know it will be difficult for you to understand, and that you will probably hate me, but sometimes things change.

I hope one day you will realise, dear Marta, that I **had** to leave. I had no choice. People change accidentally, and I changed, and so did Mum without us even noticing. Mum and

I wanted different things, but we **both** want the best for you, Marta, we really do.

I enclose a parcel, something special. I really hope you will learn to forgive me. In the parcel is a modern telescope! It's much lighter than the brass one you like to carry around, and more powerful. There are good things about both. You have always been a stargazer, Marta, since you and Granddad watch together and saw comets. This one you can control via a computer. And that is the next thing I shall get you, so put the program disc safe and wish upon the stars, my little daughter!

Love always, Dad X

Chapter Twenty-Nine

Sadness!

This is possibly the worst time of my life. A letter full of riddles from Dad.

I don't think he means it. I really **don't**. I think he's tired and hungry from driving lorries. I think if he had a bacon sandwich he could think straight. I think he'd realise it was just a passing thought, not wanting to come home. He would realise his heart belonged at home, not in France…the place that's sunny but has no real "family" in it.

I don't know what to think. I hate Mum right now. She works **all** the time, and I have to watch Quiz Shows with Tracy who never changes her socks or tracksuits.

Why can't Dad understand that I don't **really** want a Swing Coat, or red shiny shoes or a telescope to see the Stars?

I only want **one** thing for my birthday. I want my Daddy to come home, walk through the door and tell me that the letter was a bad dream. A bad dream!

It must be **all my fault**. It must be my bad behaviour… asking for coats and things I don't need. Maybe Dad found out about the misunderstanding with Mr Benitez? Maybe Dad found out about me pretending I lived at Linty Wynd.

The thing is, I don't like the **real World**. I think it's cold and cruel.

Chapter Thirty

Scrimshaw Work

I went to school today with my head held down, admiring the paving stones. I walk inside the playground with a heavy heart. I feel like Dad's letter was a bolt from the blue, like a comet. Maybe it's not real. Maybe another letter will arrive inside my birthday card with **good** news.

I don't want to play today. I'm too tired. Teachers always expect you to **want** to play outside…but I – don't – want – to.

I feel angry and defiant today. Gi-Gi Sanchez waves and smiles at me, and I ignore her. It feels good. Bobby is playing marbles on the steps outside the school office. I don't really want to explain to Bobby why I don't want to join in. It's too difficult.

I pretend I need the toilet to get away and hide the fact I've been crying. I don't go to the toilet though. I notice that the "Janitor's Den" is open. It is usually locked.

I decide to seize the opportunity and look inside. It is painted beige and chocolate brown and smells of drains, old murky drains. Vibrating copper pipes are exposed on the wall and it is smaller than I expected. Mr Winston's flask is on the table. He must be busy.

Then, I don't know why I do it…but I seize an opportunity. There is a lighter next to his flask. It is silver with a black outlined ship etched on a raised cream background. It has one of those lids that clink open and shut. The picture is a ferry from olden times I feel sure. This would look good on my dressing table next to my other ferry pictures. A ferry to bring Dad back to London.

It is a must have item and **I must** make it mine. It's obviously not mine to begin with. It doesn't belong to me… but I take it – because I can. I take it…because it adds to my collection, and makes me feel closer to Dad. Janny won't notice. He's probably got plenty of lighters…but I've got only one Dad.

I pretend to Mr Green that I feel sick, so I get to go home. Mum collects me from Mr MacKenzie-Brown's office. She asks me if I'm upset. She asks me if I want to talk. I turn my face away. I don't want to sign except to Dad. I blame Mum for everything. She used to complain about the black smoke from the Ford Cortina, and that she had all the responsibility for me. Would Mum have said that if I was a perfect hearer?

Back home Mum tells me to rest so that I will be fit for school tomorrow. This suits me – I can't wait to arrange my new property on my dressing table. I'm going to pack my suitcase and find Dad in France. I just have to plan my **escape**!

Chapter Thirty-One

Daydream

I pour out my Rainy Day Jar and there is less than ever in it. Not enough to sail to France, confiscate my Dad, and take him to the coast with palm trees that stay frozen in time (and stay unswerving even by the grandest hurricanes).

On Saturday, I will walk to the Thames and hitchhike on boats going to France. I shall begin collecting food for the journey and to share with the ship's captain who will let me take the wheel on the bridge. Nan liked bridge rolls with potted meat. I hate potted meat. It's all jellied in texture and looks like frogspawn, or something unidentified that you would find in a rock pool.

I will take jam sandwiches, a bottle of Red Cola and a serviette to wipe my mouth so it doesn't have red stains on it from the Cola and jam.

When I get to France I will need a place to stay and a job. I might be a kid, but I can work hard and learn fast. I think being able to prepare fish will mean that I can get a job in a kitchen. The French eat massive amounts of horses, frogs, snails and **fish**. I can now dress crabs which doesn't involve speaking to them or putting them in waistcoats as I once thought. Some of those chefs that have travelled The Seven Seas need a kitchen wench what can fetch and carry.

Chapter Thirty-Two

Stalled Carousel!

Today at school seemed a lot of white lies rolled into a candyfloss. If school is a fairground, then I am the carousel that does not turn around and around. I am the carousel that is stuck, making a grinding noise. The carousel that is empty. With disappointed children standing around clutching their useless fares. With Dads glaring bitterly at the flummoxed engineers who are covered in black grease and embarrassment.

Mr Green is worried. He sits me at the front of the classroom near his desk. He signs, "what has happened to my bony girl?" I hope he means "bonny".

"I – feel – sick."

Mr Green says that if I do not feel better within the hour he will ask Mr MacKenzie-Brown to call my mum.

Why all the fuss? Why do they have to contact the parents? Why can't I just go home by myself? It's all so stupid and unnecessary.

I decide it's better to stay at school and try to blank out things about Dad, than go home and face a million dollar question from Mum (again). Mum obviously feels guilty about working all the time, and leaving me with Tracy the neighbour who has the common sense of a garden spade and sends me out for scratch cards, scratches them furiously with her false nails and looks daggers at me when she doesn't win.

Tracy spends so much time watching Quiz Shows she should be a genius by now. Unfortunately for me, that is not the case. She makes me a cheese and pickle sandwich and leaves out the cheese.

The sooner I get to France, the better. Maybe I can sleep in Dad's lorry but I read a book about a mouse that found a Victorian Town House empty. The mouse lived in there with a cupboard full of bread and cheese, and lived the life of Riley.

I think that if I take my broken "lucky" brooch and turn on the spot three times anti-clockwise I might find dozens of fifty-pound notes.

Chapter Thirty-Three

Hudsons

The sum in my Rainy Day Jar means that I can travel to (wait for it!) the library! That is not **exactly** what I had in my vision of a new life as "Miss Marta G. Ziegler, Professional Parisian Photographer and Inventor Extraordinaire".

Back to my alternative plan AKA Plan B. My mermaid dress. Mr Green **is** a kindred spirit. I **will** continue with my Invention Book and making my mermaid dress. It will take my mind off things.

I've started making some sketches in pencil. Rough drawings and lots of styles. I have my first design with a fitted bodice encrusted with tiny razor shells and a fish tail which swirls as you walk. It honestly does not resemble the black bin bag. Not in any way at all. It looks like gold dust. It looks like the kind of dress that a mermaid would wear to an Awards Ceremony, or on an Oceanic Cruise.

My second design is quite tricky. It is a shorter dress, which reveals the mermaid's tail – which I will make with lots of silver foil. My dress is covered in seaweed. I know that doesn't sound very attractive...but it really looks magical. The bottle green dangly pieces of seaweed and bracken are lit by hand sewn sequins.

I think Mr Green will not believe his eyes. He does not strike me as the kind of teacher who would appreciate fashion design – he wears green tartan socks. Yet I think he might smile and maybe display my work at the Assembly on Friday morning. I live in hope!

I'm going to Mrs Viney's tonight. She has a brilliant sewing box with absolutely everything in it…pearly buttons, sparkly sequins, squares of polka-dot fur, fancy scissors that cut your fabric with zigzag edges. I cannot wait!

I have discovered a new treasure. Mrs Hudson's shop is curved at the front with a door that has diamond shaped glass. It looks like a ginger bread house. The curved window has a criss-cross design like icing sugar. The window has the most wonderful display of treasure that would brighten any dull day.

Candy sticks fall in spirals wrapped around silver fairy lights. A tiny house made of liquorice sits nestled on the window ledge with a chimney made of coconut cream, and a path made of pure vanilla fudge. There are even chocolate dancing figures that skate!

Mrs Hudson has overflowing glass jars of every sweet that ever was invented. Jars of pink sugar mice with fine string tails, and real treacle toffee that sticks to your teeth (in the best kind of way). Mrs Viney likes the pure honeycomb bar. She says it is like the taste of her childhood. Mrs Viney talks in riddles sometimes. I laugh when she smashes up the bar of honeycomb into tiny pieces with a rolling pin and throws it over a big bowl of homemade ice cream. She says it's like being back home in Dublin.

Chapter Thirty-Four

The Bridge

My mermaid dress has begun to be invented! My tailor's dummy (which I have called Genevieve for fun!) is sitting in the back shop of The Magenta Lobster in our secret room. Mrs Viney says, "Get your head out of the clouds." Mrs Viney is so practical sometimes. As there is only another week to go, I **have** to get the mermaid dress finished.

The good thing is that Genevieve the tailor's dummy stands still – which is just as well. Black bin bags are trickier to work with than you might imagine. They **do** tear a lot if you are heavy handed. I will have to be more delicate.

I have washed all the razor shells and seaweed in a colander and they look just perfect. Making the fish tail of the mermaid is "ambitious to the point of silly," according to Mrs Viney. Mrs Viney has a good plan. She is allowing me to cut up her old petticoats. We will then dye them blue and will stick some lentils and split peas on to the blue petticoats to look like fish scales. I think it will look great under the spotlights in the classroom.

I am really enjoying this project. Mr Green gave us a good lesson showing us an example of being an Inventor. He took three bricks and linked them together with a rope. He then told us a story about a gypsy family that were not allowed to live in their caravan on the empty field. They were outsiders.

They were not welcome. They were always moving on…never forgetting their roots…living simply.

Mr Green then lifted up the bricks and string and asked us what they **represented**? Bobby wrote "Home" on the board. Georgia Deevy wrote "Possessions". Gi-Gi Sanchez wrote, "Castle".Then in a flash…I put my hand up. I wasn't sure if it was the right answer, but I thought I would give it a try.

"A rope bridge of pygmy cannibals," I said.

Mr Green tapped his watch and asked for the time. "Now write down your reasons for homework," he told us.

In my Inventor Diary I wrote about my mermaid dress.

"The reason that I chose to invent a dress for a mermaid is that I wanted to use my Imagination. I believe mermaids are powerful and magical because we know they are there, lurking on the ocean bed. We cannot see them perhaps, but we can sense them. I suppose I chose mermaids because they are different, they don't quite fit into what you expect of them. They are free spirits that can swim away, and dance in the water to their own tune."

I cannot **hear** like the others in the class…but I can **sense** things. I **know** when someone is truly in trouble, or saying something behind my back. I don't need to read their lips. I can just **feel** it.

Mrs Viney says that I have "intuition". I suppose that's a tricky word for people who have to have everything pointed out to them. I've enjoyed being an Inventor, because it's allowed me to dream a little. I think dreaming is the most important thing in the World. As well as Imagination.

My Dad says that too many people want to stamp on an Imagination, like it's **wrong**. It's like they are scared of what they don't understand.

I think Dad is right.

Chapter Thirty-Five

I Decide to Write Back to Dad

I look at Dad's letter again and something is mulling over and over in my mind. I can't help but notice that the postmark is not from France. The address doesn't look French and it doesn't say Angleterre on the envelope to me. I look at the stamp again. Maybe Dad is going to **surprise** me by coming to visit the house on my birthday. I ask Mum.

She pretends she is distracted poaching eggs. I ask Mum again if Dad is coming home. This time she leaves the eggs to their fate over the simmering water. "No, Marta," is the quick reply.

I think Mum should be trying harder to get Dad back. I don't feel like my poached egg on toast. I would rather go to Mrs Viney's. It's funny. I know Dad said in his letter that there was money to buy a Swing Coat and shoes for my birthday. But they don't feel so exciting anymore. It doesn't feel that they will turn me into somebody grand.

I think I would only **hide** behind the Swing Coat and scarlet shoes. I would be able to imagine that I lived in Linty Wynd, but I would still be back with the Mums with prams huddled together on the communal brick wall.

The Swing Coat doesn't seem important at all. I think I'll keep my navy anorak. It suits Flick, and it suits me. **I shall** open the telescope on my birthday, though. Telescopes are about hope, and excitement and travels to the Stars. I now have two, so my chances are doubled!

I will write to Dad without Mum knowing. Mums only spoil things. They want you to stop asking questions. It makes their life easier. They want you to stop playing with ferrets because they think ferrets are dirty and dangerous. Most of all, they want you to **change** for all the wrong reasons.

Chapter Thirty-Six

Letter to Dad

Dear Dad,

I thought I would write to thank you for my birthday money. I cannot wait to open the telescope. Maybe you could show me how it works when you next come back on the ferry.

I really want you to come home soon, Dad, because I have been working hard at school and trying hard, just like you asked. I am trying harder than ever to get a Gold Star...and I think I may be able to get one this time.

I am making a mermaid's dress and it is really exciting. I will take photographs to show you. I'll save having a birthday cake until you get home, Dad. I really don't mind. I can't make a wish unless you are here.

I know you said people can **change**, Dad, and so can I (honestly). I can be a good girl. **I promise**.

Please, Daddy, read this letter. **Please**.

I miss you, and I hate poached eggs.

Your Lonely Daughter,

Marta   ☹   x

Chapter Thirty-Seven

No Answer

Four weeks from sending my letter to Dad, and no reply. Easy, it might have got lost in the post. I wrote **another** letter with better words **and** a drawing of my mermaid's dress. **Six** weeks! Still no reply. Dad **must** be **so** busy.

I keep checking the mat under the letterbox every day with hope.

Hope is a good word, **isn't it**?

Chapter Thirty-Eight

I See Dad!

Mum sent me to the supermarket today. I **hate** going to the supermarket by myself. It's like a **maze**, and you can't find anything. Mum sent me for half a dozen eggs and gave me **enough** money, so that was fine.

It was then that I realised that things **do change**, like a whirlwind…a hurricane that you cannot control. I took the wrong way in the supermarket. I was too busy looking at the displays of sunflowers and fancy tubs of marguerites.

Anyway, if I hadn't stopped to look at the flowers, I would never have noticed the photograph that I would **never** have taken. You see, the flowers were next to the fruit and veg… nothing too exciting you might think. That is except I saw someone I never **expected** to see.

Right in front of me as if in a haze of mist…I saw **my Dad**. It was him all right: tall, smiling and happier than he had ever looked before.

Dad wasn't alone. I couldn't quite take it in, and grasp what I was seeing. Dad was pushing a supermarket trolley with a baby girl in the seat! She had blonde hair, and was dressed in pink from head to toe. She looked perfect.

As I stood staring, as if there was nobody else that mattered, I realised Daddy was not alone with the baby girl. A woman with her back to me brushed Dad's hand, and put a pineapple in the trolley.

The lady didn't look like my Mum. She looked younger, and was wearing a hat that tilted slightly on her head. I was just watching...and just watching is the hardest thing of all.

I noticed something else, something important. Dad was **not signing** to the girl. He was **mouthing** words, he was! I think that means what I don't want to imagine **ever**. I think that Dad has a **replacement** baby girl that **can hear**. A baby girl that will grow up to be the way Dad wants her to be.

As I stand watching I don't understand what is happening at all. Is Dad getting married again? Why had Dad forgotten Mum and me?

Why? I needed an answer, but at that moment I was in despair. I **couldn't** ask. I just stood hiding behind the tins of beans that were shaped into a six-foot pyramid.

At that moment, with me trembling, Flick threw herself forward sensing my trouble and knocking down the entire bean pyramid.

I was hot and angry. Dad had a baby girl. I had a sister I didn't know! Why? I believed Dad all of this time and now I was sorry that I had...not telling me this was as bad as lying, wasn't it?

Chapter Thirty-Nine

Mum to the Rescue!

Seeing Dad meant that I had a secret. I wasn't telling Mum. She is far too busy at Mr Deevy's office. I don't even tell Mrs Viney. I tell no one, not a soul. It hurts too much. Tomorrow is my birthday, and I don't care. I really don't.

I decide to take drastic action. I decide to start being **me**, Marta G. Ziegler – making her own decisions! I decide not to go to school today. I can pretend I feel sick again, easily. I know that Mrs Viney will be going to the fish market today. So now is a good time.

I decide to **take** the mermaid's dress (that is nearly finished) away from the secret room at the Magenta Lobster. I decide to take it…because I don't want to finish it. I decide to take it… because I don't want to go back to school.

I take the mermaid's dress off the tailor's dummy and carry it away over my arm. I decide to take it to the empty play park and hide it in the concrete tunnels. It's a good, safe and easy hiding place.

As I crawl inside the tunnel, I tear the razor shells and seaweed off the dress. After all, it's not a "proper dress". It's all make believe. It is all worthless.

I smash the razor shells hard against the concrete, one at a time…I then rip the black bin bag, tearing it with my fists. I don't **want** a gold star anymore. Who cares? As I rip up the

94

seaweed with my gritty hands, I feel like a **destroyer**, not an **inventor**. **I feel good**. I feel **in control**. Dads only **cheat and lie!**

As I continue to cry, a face peered into the tunnel. It was Mum. She was going to be angry.

Instead, Mum took me gently by the hand and **smiled**. "Running away?" she asked.

I nodded.

"Me too," she said. "No work today," Mum added. I could tell Mum had been crying too because she was smiling too broadly and her eyes were red.

Mum leaned on the outside of the tunnel, and told me that she had known all the time about Dad. She explained that she had tried to protect me, but she was wrong in trying to do so. Mum then explained that she still **loved** Dad, but he did not feel the same. He had felt "trapped" and Mum had thought it best to let him go. Mum then said that she was going to give up the typing job at Mr Deevy's because it meant less time with me.

"Money is helpful, but **you** come first, second and third," she said. Mum thinks that Tracy the neighbour is not "a good influence" on me. When I show Mum the remains of the mermaid's dress, she is not angry. Again, I am surprised.

We go to Mrs Hudson's sweet shop for a curly ice cream and Mum says that she will enjoy making a new dress with me. As we walk home together eating our ice creams, I realise that I have not always been fair to Mum. She didn't **lie** to **hurt** me, she **lied** to **help** me be happy.

My name is Marta G. Ziegler...and for the first time I realise that Mum loves me for **who** I am. If you have one person that loves you despite everything, **then** you can be anyone you want to be.

I got a Gold Star! I got a it for the mermaid's dress and story. Mr Green gave me my certificate in front of the class, and **everyone** stood up and clapped for me. I didn't feel happy, though, because I knew Dad didn't care.

The certificate read,

"Marta has shown a great deal of imagination in writing about mermaids."

I knew all along that Mr Green was a kindred spirit. But the good feeling didn't last long. Now that I had the Gold Star, I didn't want it anymore.

I hated it.

Maybe if I had been good, better – Dad would never have met this woman younger than Mum.

I threw my gold star into a puddle. It was bad luck.

Chapter Forty

The Journey
(The Pretending Game)

Now that I know the truth about Dad, Mum seems to look at me more…instead of glancing away.

She has told me things will be **different** from now on. Different **good**, not different **bad**. I'll never complain about the smell from Dad's Ford Cortina again. If Dad came home to live all the time I would eat the meat and potato pie (with the soggy pastry) that he used to buy from the corner shop.

Maybe that is why Dad left in the first place…because I used to mash the meat and potatoes with my fork. Sometimes you don't realise that you can annoy other people, but you do. Then adults get angry like a firework shooting into the sky with splinters of colour. Yes, angry like a firecracker.

I'm going to draw a firework in my diary for Mr Green. If I was to describe myself as a firework, I would be a Catherine Wheel. I like to know where I am going…even if it's in circles. Round and Round. Showering out coloured sparks while people whoop and clap!

We have to "downsize" to an estate called Z Place. I – I can't let Mum know how I feel about leaving this house. I need to smile with snappier smiles like Flick (then Mum will be relieved).

The new flat is going to be like living on top of a mountain.

It won't have a garden. It won't have many windows, but it will be like a new adventure. Maybe.

You know when you are upset, but can't let on. I…I wanted to show Mum that I didn't need anybody (except her and Flick). I – wanted to – pretend. Yes, I thought the flat was different (bad), not different (good).

There is no front door, just a corridor leading to stairs… though I saw a black cat and I think that's lucky. The smell was strong. The kind of smell of a car park outside, with lots of rubbish strewn around. I stepped inside, and imagined the corridor and stairs to be a rope-bridge leading to a tree house.

As I climbed the stairs (the lift had a mattress stuffed into it which smelt like a toilet. This was disappointing.), I imagined that I was a racoon – or something interesting like that. Racoons run quickly, and are inquisitive like I am. Mum walked slowly…she'll get used to the stairs, with time!

We are at the top of the tree house. Number 120. This is it. The turquoise door is a little bit faded…but it would have been like a jewel, when it was new and shiny in William the Conqueror's time.

Mum sits slumped at the kitchen window. I know what she's thinking, but I play the "pretending" game. The kitchen is so small, it is a great hiding place for a racoon. The bathroom is a strange colour with orange patterned wallpaper covered with parrots. The kind of wallpaper that you would see in a café in Hawaii or somewhere like that. I wonder if you get jammy doughnuts in Hawaii…

The grand tour took less than ten seconds, but that means it is a friendly place. As I think about being a racoon again (because Mum is crying), I notice that the big living room window has a view of concrete, grey gravel and more concrete.

I put my hand on Mum's shoulder and sign, " A tree house. Sky!"

Mum suddenly smiles. This house high in the sky, where you can look down on barbed wire fences, and a park without swings…is a window to the World. **My** window to the World, and a new adventure.

It **has** to be! I have no choice, do I?

Chapter Forty-One

Party at Bloomsbury Square
(Snow and Ice in my Heart)

"Noella de Coeur and family cordially invite Miss Marta G. Ziegler to a Winter Celebration in Honour of Noella's 10th Birthday."

The invitation was on proper card that didn't buckle in your hand, and the writing was in curly calligraphy with glimmering gold around the edge.

I showed it to Mrs Viney. She was quiet. She looked at the invitation and considered it.

"Marta, remember not to forget that you come from Z Place. You would be going into a World you don't understand, and where they don't understand you. Z Place may not have grandeur but you are **safe** there."

I didn't want Z Place with smashed up glass bottles in the playground and no ambition. I wanted to be like Noella de Coeur, Gi-Gi Sanchez and the other girls that looked better than me.

Bobby McGonigal asked if I was going to the party. "Marta, Noella is trouble. Maybe you shouldn't go. I wouldn't think any less of you."

That was an outrage! What did Bobby McGonigal mean? How could he say that? I **would** go with my head held **high**.

Noella was doing a talk at school about her birthday party

(with slides). Lucky **us** to be the audience with 120 slides of what she wanted for her 10th birthday, with many pictures of horses. Mr Green sat at the back craftily eating out of his tin and sipping Scotch.

I put my head on my desk. I'd had enough.

Bobby jolted my desk and passed me a note. "Don't go to the party, Marta, better stay away. Just in case…"

Bobby had overstepped the mark this time. I would **not** be told what to do or think. Who did he think he was telling me not to go to a party that everyone in the class was invited to? His uncle was a psychologist and was stupid. Bobby was the same. I wrote, "Go away!"

Now, this was my plan. I would search the markets to make something to wear for the birthday party. I would cut and sew it myself, and it would be unique. I went to the library, taking Flick, to look up some ideas.

I'd never actually been to a public library before but I knew they would have pictures in books…at least I hoped they might. Z place didn't have a library, but three bus stops away there was such a place. It was old, had a smell of musty books and huge magical windows that you might see in a Scottish Castle. You could imagine a dungeon in this library!

I spun around in a figure of eight looking at the height of the bookshelves and the enormity of the stone walls. I was sure there was a secret corridor leading to jewels, hidden diamonds and treasures.

I wrote on a piece of paper "Coco Bonheur Chanel".

A lady with silvery hair and sparkly eyes beckoned me to a bookcase. It was crammed with lots of books about Coco Chanel. I could hear in my head what she asked. "You like Coco?"

I signed, "I want to be like her." I'd forgotten that not everyone knows Sign.

The librarian replied in Sign, "She was surely magical, good luck young lady."

I spent every night after school with pencil and paper and the drawing books Nan bought me – drawing my ideas. I looked at the drawings by Coco, and then made them simple for me. I was not in Paris. I was in Z Place, but that did not matter. I drew, and drew and drew…until the drawing books were full.

I was ready. The Librarian who was always smiling tapped me on the arm. It was school time and I had decided to skip more of Noella's slides and thought she was going to ask me why I wasn't at school.

"I thought of you and wondered if you would like these as a gift. Your drawings are very good!"

The silvery haired Librarian handed me several huge brown paper bags that had a smell of oranges and pomegranates. I tentatively opened them and inside was every fabric you could dream of folded up like a concertina. Black and mauve chiffon, brocades, velvet and tweeds.

I knew it was expensive, and looked in my pocket. I had return fare money and string. I offered all I had in my pocket to the lady. "I can pay more next Tuesday," I signed.

"This is a **gift**. Everyone needs a chance and, if you follow me, there is a study room with a table."

I was led through to a huge room with fancy oil paintings on the wall and high ceilings.

"You can work here in peace."

I didn't know what to say. I thought for a moment. "I wondered why you would help **me**?"

The Librarian looked me in the eye. "The way you looked when you found those books meant I **had** to help you. My Grandfather was a tailor in Italy. He knew your Nan…your Nan was stylish."

I didn't know what to say, but I thought I should tell the truth. "I do not think I deserve the room. I have a social worker called Natasha because they think I'm bad and stupid. They might take me away from Mum one day. They plan my future and nobody believes in me, except Flick."

The lady smiled. "One day you will astound them all!"

I had made a friend in the library. Her name was Seraphina. I began work not only on my dress for the party, but also on a jacket, made from the tweed, for Seraphina.

However, disaster struck. Natasha the social worker crawled into the library. She looked angry, and like a warrior. She used Sign language with a bossy flourish.

"You have not been attending school, Marta Ziegler! You do not **care**, do you? I have the power to make big changes for you, Miss. Your time is running out! You show defiance to a psychologist, but no longer! You will learn that bad behaviour leads to ruin. Climbing on the school roof and refusing to come down demands!"

I had picketed myself on the school roof when I had been cheated out of a Story Prize due to a silly formality. I have written down this "escapade" as it was called in another diary.

Seraphina signed to Natasha, "This is a **library**. Can I help you?"

Natasha sneered. "I am taking this client home. So I can assess her. She has become a sneak thief. She needs assessment!"

Sneak thief? What other kinds are there? Am I supposed to hire a trumpet player to go before me like the Pharisee spoken of by Our Lord?

Seraphina signed back, "I don't know why we are still signing Miss Dostoevsky, but Marta works here. Please don't take away her happiness!"

"Marta has issues and her behaviour needs ironing out. She is a truant, and I will see her at nine tomorrow in the Headmaster's office if she wishes to avoid dire consequences!"

She turned and left the library, shaking off Flick who had her by the heel and then turning to sign Naughty Words at the ferret!

I turned towards the stacks and signed Naughty Words of my own.

Seraphina twisted me to face her. Her eyes were full of laughter and she hugged me.

The day had arrived, and my hands were so eager to wave to everyone at Z Place, I lost all sense of time. I had only half an hour to get ready for the party. I wanted to show Bobby McGonigal that no one was going to tell me what to do.

In the library, I had looked at lots of pictures that looked tea-stained…old pictures of black and white Movie Stars. I borrowed Nan's old red lipstick and had my hair in bits of old tea towel. Eadie in the flat below knew that putting your hair in rags made you look a million dollars. Eadie used to work in the fishmongers near the Jazz Club, so she would know.

Eadie surprised me by presenting me with a dusty old box, that had seen better days, wrapped in lots of old newspaper. I reluctantly opened the box to find the most amazing pair of scarlet soft leather shoes with a little heel. I could not believe that such a shabby, torn box could contain something so beautiful.

Eadie had a tear in her eye. I tried the shoes on and twirled around, so excited, but could see Eadie turn away.

There was a story that Eadie had met a Man from New York who gave her red dancing shoes , with the carrier bag and everything. They had gone dancing for one night , and she never saw him again. Nan told me the story and was not allowed to tell anyone because it was "private business".

Eadie smiled and pointed at me to hold out my hand. I did so, and Edie pressed a little silver mirror into it. At that moment, I felt just as good as any of the other girls. I was invincible!

My dress and little jacket sewn with so much hope and care shimmered in the slate sky. I carefully placed the invitation in my handbag, safe to hold at the door.

I clicked the heels of the red shoes tree times for luck and ran down the stairs of the apartment block where all the neighbours stood waving at me. I felt like someone really important. A girl from Z place going to the London Pavillion!

Finally, my big moment arrived…I arrived at the London Pavillion strews with ice-blue fairy lights. It was magical!

Noella's Dad was dressed in a fancy suit with a bow tie, and suddenly I felt very, very stupid. All the girls were in long dresses to the floor except me. They had something like a flower corsage on their wrists and I looked different.

I smiled. The girls stared and sniggered. I had left a safety pin on my dress and a tiny piece of thread dangled from my waist. I could see more broad smiles.

I looked at the gold invitation which suddenly looked blurry, and I tried to avoid the girls that looked like wolves.

There were ice sculptures of ballerinas and fish on silver platters with the eyes still bulging; vegetables carved like roses, and tall towers of cupcakes.

Noella's Dad unexpectedly could Sign. He asked:

"You are from Z place ? Good to see you." I could not believe he knew where I came from , so I lied.

"No, not me."

I thought of somewhere… "I live in a big house with a blue door, and a big garden with a gate with no concrete at all."

Noella's Dad looked at me thoughtfully. "I used to live in Z Place."

I could not believe what had just happened. Noella de Coeur's Dad came from Z place? How could that be? I made sure I got away quickly and looked at the curtains instead… they were sparkled with little gems, sparkling stones as if from a treasure chest. I pulled my dress down to look longer and tried to eat a few sandwiches that I could find (that I knew what they were). I did not want to be allergic…

The party was unforgettable. I stood by myself, an outsider, watching. I would never be at such a place again so wanted to enjoy every moment.

I imagined as I stood hiding by the curtain that I was

blowing out the birthday candles of the biggest multi-coloured cake with sparklers I had ever seen. I imagined it was me, and that I was popular. I imagined things would one day be different to where I was living now.

I would never forget Noella's Party. Bobby McGonigal was right. I was going into a world I did not understand , and I did not like it at all.

Chapter Forty-Two

The Spanish Inquisition

In the Headmaster's Office the following morning, Mr MacKenzie-Brown apologised on her behalf for Natasha Dostoevsky's absence. She was attending at her GP's.

"Nothing serious, I hope?" I signed back, relieved and lying.

"A tetanus injection, Marta. Do you have any comment?"

"Why does she want to add tetanus to her other issues?" I replied.

"I will deal with your impertinence later, Miss. But we have to go to the hall now – I have ordered an extraordinary assembly."

Extraordinary? With elves and hobbits? I was excited and didn't pull away when the Headmaster took my hand. I was soon to have more excitement than I knew what to do with!

The entire school were settling into their seats. The teachers were on the stage and Mr MacKenzie joined them. Gregor Green was standing at the front of the podium so that his Signing could be seen.

Winston the ancient Janitor was also on the stage and, on invitation, he came forward and made an appeal for the return of an item of sentimental value taken from his Den while he was mowing the grass. Crikey! It was a steel lighter with ivory engraved "scrimshaw work". It was given to him by a good friend, having got it engraved. He did not want any punishment, but would appreciate the use of it once more before he was "called to jam with the choir angelic".

Rosina Dashwood, the Games Mistress, removed a large handkerchief from her tracksuit and began weeping into it. Winston turned to her, and although now shaking with emotion on his own account, managed to comfort her with "no woman, no cry" – obligingly signed to the assembly by a red faced Mr Green. He looked like he would prefer to comfort her himself.

Meanwhile, I felt my own face throbbing and glowing so warmly that I felt I would melt the metal fixings on the gym equipment. There occurred a mass production of strawberry straws, scooby doos, ancient conkers, red bills, wine gums and bad coin (and even worse from the pupils) as people fished for something to weep with.

Hypocritically, I felt in my jacket pocket, and to my horror, almost pulled out the property in question which I had taken to carrying for its comforting weight. The lid had closed on my hanky.

Everyone was now crying at such a sad parting of an old man and his memories. I hid my face under my hanky and bellowed with the best of them – until I realised that a hushed silence had fallen. It seemed that all eyes were on me.

A dry eyed and very impatient Mr MacKenzie-Brown signed and spoke at the same time. "This is all very well but which one of you little..." a cough from Ms Dashwood "... little scholars lifted this item? I will allow one week, one **working** week. We are obviously in the presence of a master hypocrite. The matter will be closed, if the item is restored by Friday. We will allow this very **materious** matter to remain between the Culprit and his or her Creator, and the Master. After the hymn we will RTU."

The Headmaster was a major in the Royal Army Educational Corp and says "Return to Unit" when he means we should get to our classrooms 'at the double'.

He then nodded to Mr Rossini B.Mus (Hons), Ms Dashwood's pianist who accompanied us as we sang "Oh Lord and Master of Mankind, Forgive Our Foolish Ways, Restore us to our Rightful Mind…"

I watched, recovering and entranced, as Mr McKenzie-Brown's jaw bounced up and down. He has got, according to Mr Green, a "fine baritone voice.". He can get his index, middle and ring finger in his mouth all at once and vertically without breaking his jaw. He tells us this every morning but this time we went straight into the hymn, missing the tra-la-la-ing, hey nonny no-ings, diaphragm tortures and mass coughing that is our usual "warm up".

On Thursday, the day before the McKenzie-Brown Ultimatum (I had waited as I did not want to be caught returning the item – this would be as bad as having been caught taking it and there were bound to be curious cats creeping around), I again found the Den door open – as one would have expected.

I looked for the last time at the engraving "To Winston from Bob" and polishing the lovely thing on my sleeve (I do not want to give my dee and ay to the police state), placed it on the desk next to the flask. I noticed the flask for the first time, it was silver and looked like it was something from a stately home, and it had a silver plate attached – bearing the same dedication. It would have sent Mr Winston to jam with the Archangels straight away and for sure. This would have made me "Marta Ziegler – Artist, Inventor and Master Thief".

The two items looked vulnerable; but I knew I had to stop playing games that would hurt Mum. I was glad when I closed the door behind me and I felt the lock click. Standing outside, I felt a tremor from the floor which moved through my shoes. As though someone was dancing a hornpipe behind the door.

I hope he doesn't celebrate by smoking and drinking himself to death! Crikey and God Bless!

Though who **am** I to even **think** about God!

Chapter Forty-Three

Amber and the New Baby
(and Me)

Mr Green says it is important to write things down – **what** you think, **why** you think it. Like a journey. Mr Green says it should be fun. I think it is not as fun as drawing or making things.

Mr Green is acting as if he is enthusiastic about this by saying we can decorate the diary with anything we want. To make it special. You know…important to **us**.

I have decided to keep my cover **blank**, until I can think of something good. Something exciting – in a good way. Not like recent adventures.

I know what I **don't** want on the cover. I **don't** want a picture of new baby Sophia. I also **don't** want a photograph of Dad with Amber, his new "friend", or whatever she is. Amber is the name of a treasured substance from trees – something that brings you luck (except for the insects sometimes trapped in it). What luck has she brought my Mum? She's more bad luck…like a lump of coal.

Amber will be my new step-Mum and I will have to pretend, and hide like I am a Jack in the Box.

I don't believe that I need a step-Mum. I already have a non-step Mum. It's like building a giant pyramid from jigsaw pieces that are taped together. Forced. Stuck. A puzzle that can't fit together, and so building it, as if it can, is silly…stupid.

Mum says she is over the moon about Dad's new baby, Sophia. I don't think she means it as she said it through gritted teeth.

When I was little I wanted a little brother or sister (when Mum and Dad were happy) but it never happened. I wished for it every day.

What did Mr Green say on the board when we were writing stories? "Be careful what you wish for."

I don't know exactly what he meant, but maybe today, I do! I wonder if Dad will love Sophia more than he loves me, because she can hear? I wonder…maybe I'll never know… because Dad would never tell the truth about that, would he?

When I grow up I won't marry once, never mind twice! I am just going to live by myself with Flick the Ferret.

Chapter Forty-Four

Diary of Marta Z None

If Mr Green wants a diary, then so be it. I can only try my best!

Today I wrote something "wrong" in my diary. I wrote that I wished that Amber would step on an aeroplane and never come back! I wrote it in big letters (**over** the jotter line in **big** capital letters). That means that I really must have meant it!

Amber is not what I drew in the picture for Mum to see. Amber is younger than Mum, I think. Her blonde hair, with no black roots showing, frames a face that is always simpering. Yes, to make things even more unlucky, Amber grins like a cheetah, and I think her teeth are fake. They are far too straight.

Bobby says that Amber's Dad owns a garage. A garage that **sells** and **fixes** cars. My Dad will like that and maybe that's the only reason her likes Amber...because her Daddy owns so many cars!

Mum used to say to him, "Why don't you marry that Cortina? You spend more time with it than with me!"

Bobby says that the garage sales room has two big scarlet soft sofas that you can squash your hands into, and it leaves a shape and your ands smelling of leather. It also has a vending machine that makes cups of tea, coffee and chicken noodle soup.

It sounds silly, like Dad .What can I do to make him see

sense ? I wonder when he will change his mind and come back to us with his suitcase in his hand, smiling at me.

I wonder when...

Chapter Forty-Five

The Zoo

Mum and Dad have come up with a great idea. I have to start being nice to Amber. They think it's good to get to know baby Sophia. Why, I don't know.

Amber is so excited about going to The London Zoo to see the Penguin Beach! This is a nightmare. I need to think quickly, very quickly to get out of this one!

Hey Presto! I decide that I have "inherited" or got "contaminated" with Chicken Pox. I know not many people get it like a cold, but it's the best excuse I can think of. I need all the excuses I can get!

I run up and down the stairs. Up, down, up down, and twirl around. Faster and faster. I can feel my heart beating quicker and that is good. I wrap myself in a warm towel from the airing cupboard and put on the thickest socks and woolliest jumper I can find. Then I stick on a woolly hat, as if I am going to climb the most dangerous of glaciers.

It is in fact a hot day, so I look silly, but it will be worth all the effort! Then comes the best bit. I raid my art box and cover my whole face with bright red and purple felt-tip dots. All over my nose, ear lobes and hands. I wonder if they are "toxic" or "non-toxic". Right now, I can't remember what the word means.

Before I can remember, Mum bursts into my room as if she

is about to explode. Her face is aghast as if she has encountered a spider in her custard, or something worse. She is not laughing at my appearance. She is furious.

I am frog-marched to the bathroom and Mum scrapes my face with a sour, scratchy face cloth and soap that is something herbal and yucky. The felt-tip colours have gone, but my face is as red as a beetroot.

I wish I hadn't bothered going to this much trouble to avoid an outing.

To make matters worse, as I am so fond of photography, I am to record the entire trip and present the photographs as a slideshow for school.

The journey to the zoo in the Cortina is grim. It is raining, and I sit squashed beside baby Sophia in her lavender coloured car seat with her travel bag, changing mat, rattles, nappies, baby-bottles, a tin of SMF, Milton tablets, velour bottle warmer, cardboard baby books with frightening beasties and baby wipes. Baby **everything**. There is no room for Flick who has been left with her cotton mice and food in her cage. Just as well, last time the zookeepers thought she was an escapee!

I have my navy blue anorak, Nan's camera and a tripod. I do not **look** or **feel** like the Inventor or Adventurer of my dreams.

Amber has brought a picnic. She has obviously spent too much time cutting off all the crusts. They are **perfectly** triangular. They are jam and cheese. Not together. I'm hungry, but pretend that I am not. It takes more than a sandwich to impress me. Amber is not going to be my new Mum, and I'm not going to hide the fact.

My lip reading is getting better and quicker. I am trying to concentrate, and watch without staring. It's tricky.

I didn't watch the penguins for long. I took pictures, turned my back and then wandered off to look at the giraffes. Giraffes feel a bit like me. They can **watch** over people…and can see more than any other animal in the zoo.

115

They probably don't need to **hear**, they just **watch**.

Amber tried to take my hand in the souvenir shop, but I deliberately let go. I don't want to **try** – I just don't.

When we arrived home at last, Amber was crying with Dad. I could read what she was saying. I could see it clearly. Right now, I just want to go home with Mum. I didn't take many photographs of the zoo but some of the rainbow in the overcast sky.

Chapter Forty-Six

Deadly Deevy

Mr Green says, "Adventure is Good." **Imagination** makes us travellers in time and space. It is our own personal Tardis.

Gorgeous Georgia Deevy is back to her old ways. She is now making pyramids out of pieces of paper (that you fold over) and putting a name of a person in the class next to a description. The pyramid got passed to me by Gi-Gi, and next to Bobby McGonigal's name was written the word "Blind".

I folded the pyramid over and stuck it in my tidy-tray in my desk amongst my pens. I don't want Bobby to see it. Bobby is not as strong as I am. He's not. He is also not very good at balance. That doesn't sound a big thing, but he keeps falling off his bike. The other boys laugh at him, and he laughs as well... but sometimes you do laugh when you hurt, don't you? I think so. I do!

I keep the pyramid in my tray, so that I can take it home in my satchel to read at home. I want to be **ready** to read it. I wonder what will be written next to my name?

Mr Green gives us model globes to paint, and I am not concentrating as I try to colour in the Pacific Ocean. I am thinking about how words are more hurtful than being hit with a rock.

I haven't told anyone that I have moved to a new flat...it's another three bus stops away. Somehow they know. I decide that I cannot wait until tonight to read the pyramid. While everyone is concentrating on painting, I sneak a look underneath my desk. I look for my name. I get flustered as I open the thing, my hands are shaking…

Then I find it…Marta Ziegler. My heart feels like concrete. I feel grey. I feel stupid. Georgia has drawn me with messy hair, greasy, dirty. In fact the drawing is the worst thing that I could have imagined. I am drawn digging in the school quiet garden with my bare hands and another cartoon is of me eating gravel and mud pies. Underneath the picture is written, "My name is Marta. I **smell** entirely of ferret and nick from elderly caretakers and shopkeepers."

My eyes are welling up like puddles, but I don't want to cry at school. I don't want Georgia to see me **break**. I **can't** let Georgia see me sad. She will **not** win. That's why Georgia does these things…to be the King of the Castle. That's why.

I think she must know that I live at 120 Z Place. They must **all** know I live there. Not that I care. Mum says it's not forever, so it's not. I'm not painting the globe anymore. It's pointless. I smell, so I don't want to travel.

Not today, not tomorrow. Maybe I'll feel different, but I don't think so…

I really don't think so…

Chapter Forty-Seven

Nan's Ghost

I take my navy anorak, and stick it in the bin with the rubbish. I wrap it in a poly-bag so Mum won't see. I **want** to change the way I look. I want to be different and pretty like Gi-Gi. The navy anorak is dragging me down.. When I wear a new, stylish coat I won't be pathetic Marta. I'll be **exciting** Marta.

As I sit beside the bin, and think about travelling the World and finding Adventure...

I think I can hear Nan speaking to me. She sounds cross. "You should never change **who** you are for anyone, Marta. You should be **proud** of who you are."

I spin round, hoping to see Nan, but I can only see a barbed-wire fence and a rusty tin can. I wonder if Nan was **really** talking to me, or if I just **wished** she was really here, making things better. Making things the way they **used** to be. Nan could fix anything!

Mind you, I don't think Nan could allow us to escape from Z Place...or get Amber to go around the World, or make Sophia not perfect and able to hear...

Chapter Forty-Eight

Uncle "Ludo" Jerry

Have you ever been to a Circus? Have you ever seen a tall man with a magical top hat, and turned up nose that changes shape like Pinocchio's? A man with fiery red hair that looks like a firework (and is real, not a wig)?

If you have, you have probably seen my Mum's brother – my uncle Ludo Jerry. Uncle Ludo isn't married. People in travelling circus-land don't have time to buy a toaster and put a carnation in their jacket. No, in the "proper" circus, time is precious. A proper circus with a flying trapeze, and jugglers than can throw fire on sticks and everything. Everyone in the circus smiles all the time and they wear silver and gold and fly without Angel wings.

No wonder they smile all the time…dancing and whirling and eating candyfloss while they stand on their head. I wouldn't complain. I could be the "Wonderful Mysterious Marta G. Ziegler with Felicity the Flying Ferret". That could be how I could be like Puss in Boots and fill my Wellingtons with gold.

Not everyone in Z Place appreciates Flick, but I think an audience in the circus would. I could spray my hair purple and wear charm bracelets on my ankles to make me look like I have travelled. It would be great. Flick could get her photograph taken, and I could live in a caravan and eat sausages and drink apple juice and gaze out the **big** windows…looking at the **big** circus tent that has become my work place.

Uncle Ludo is my Special uncle, even though I hardly ever see him. You see, Uncle Ludo always wanted to be a poet. I don't really know much about poets but I think they have curly hair and wear long black coats – I think. I've never met one.

Nan said another word for poet was "daft". That's when Uncle Ludo packed his bags and ran away. Mum said that he took the bus to Dublin with his birthday money and met a dancer called Marlee who was tap dancing on the cobbled streets. She wore a tunic of sea green and smiled with her eyes. Marlee Oakley was her name, and she could dance all night.

I think that Marlee said that to be a dancer you have to let your soul fly. I don't know what that means but I've met Marlee before and she taught me to hula-hoop in the car park of The Magenta Lobster.

Anyway, Marlee was giving out tickets to The Carafelli Circus that was in town. Uncle Jerry thought it was fate. He pretended he was a magician by trade by being courageous with playing cards and balancing them on his head. My Uncle Ludo believes that you have to seize every opportunity. Why a poet like him joined the circus I'm not sure, but it's all very exciting, don't you think?

Uncle Ludo always sends postcards from his travels. Maybe that's why he's called "Ludo". It's like the game, you throw the dice and travel the board.

Anyway, I couldn't eat my tea tonight because I am just the luckiest girl ever. Uncle Ludo is coming to visit Mum's new flat tomorrow! This is more exciting than Georgia's Fabergé Egg, or me taking photographs.

Uncle Ludo thinks that "deaf" and doing good at school doesn't matter. He thinks it is important to Imagine anything you want, and be anything you want to be. He has a book of poems from a well-loved "Champion of the Imagination" who rests in a London place called Bone Hill.

I am starting to think that hoping for a house in London is silly. My Rainy Day Jar is less than half full, and Mum gets worried when I write things which she calls dreams made of paper. They can get blown away...

I think Uncle Ludo will help Mum feel a bit better. He's someone you can **rely** on. Like a Guardian Angel. He seems to sense when Mum needs help – even when she doesn't ask for it. I think Uncle *likes* himself.

And this is the reason why *everyone else* likes him! When I grow up, I would like to be like Uncle Ludo Jerry who is another kindred spirit.

Chapter Forty-Nine

The Arrival of Uncle Ludo Jerry

Mum tidied the new flat, and kept tidying until **I** made the flat untidy again. I think that Mum was trying a little too hard. She even made a sherry trifle which is Uncle Ludo's favourite. I think Mum had used too much sherry, because you could smell it even when you opened the windows.

I think Mum made trifle which keeps because Uncle Ludo never arrives anywhere on time. Not ever! He needs a cuckoo clock instead of a top hat! At least, trifle can sit patiently in a fridge for minutes or hours…

Hurray! As if by magic, Uncle Ludo must have heard me complain. He turned up! He has arrived three hours late…but that doesn't matter. The number three is important in the circus. It's tradition that you have to do things in "threes": tie your shoelaces on three pairs of shoes three times; dancers spray and polish the soles of their shoes three times; and everything is checked (like the trapeze, on the count of three).

Now that I know that, Number Three is going to be my new lucky number!

Uncle Ludo brought his new friend, Lilia. I love that name…it's the kind of name that you would give to someone who flies on a magic carpet. It's very exciting, don't you think? **I** do. I wish I was called Lilia. I think Lilia is great. She has long hair (longer than mine) and she has fancy clasps in her hair that look like they are glistening with **real** diamonds. I really wish Georgia Deevy could see them. They send glittery, flickery glances of light all over the living room.

Mum puts out a plate of sandwiches (ham and corned beef – not together). Thankfully, Lilia is not a vegetarian. Mum was fretting about that.

Strangely, Lilia has brought us something for later. It's all very spooky. It's in a funny shaped terracotta dish with a pointy bit on the top. I thought that she had written that we were to have "a tangerine" – or was it "tangine"? I have no idea whatever it was but it did smell like Christmas. I didn't try any of it; it looked like a stew, but it had prunes!

Oh no, I absolutely do *not* eat prunes.

It can't be right to eat something that tastes so vile! Like you would imagine crocodile teeth to taste! No, I smiled at Lilia and Uncle Ludo…and pretended that I was full after the trifle. Truth is, I would have preferred fish and chips, but obviously, they eat "tangerines" in the circus!

Uncle Ludo showed me how to play Patience with a *very* big set of playing cards. He can shuffle the cards so fast, like a magician. Unbelievably quickly. It's exciting to watch. Mum didn't look that excited as she was yawning and reading a newspaper.

Never mind, Uncle Ludo and Lilia are brilliant. I wonder if they will ever get married – to each other, I mean. I would like that. I could be a bridesmaid and wear daisies in my hair…

Lilia gave me a present. It was a tiny trinket box in silver with a fancy, curly design engraved in the front. It looked like a Russian trinket box – the kind of box I saw in an old black and white film. I didn't see the whole film as the television ran out of money and I had to imagine the rest of the movie. The design is curled like a figure of eight, very beautiful. Inside was a tiny piece of crystallised ginger. It smells like cough medicine but it is supposed to be lucky.

I will keep this trinket box forever. Tucked inside it with the ginger was a little note from Uncle Ludo.

It made my heart jump.

"Dearest Marta, the World Awaits!"

Epilogue

Letter to New York

Noella's party made me realise that there was a big world I had not seen yet. Bobby Mc Gonigal might want to be a Dentist, but I want to do see everything.

There is a famous fashion designer in New York called Stefano Marallino. I decided to write to him:

Dear Mr Marallino,

I am Marta G. Ziegler and I was wondering if I could work with you in New York.

I go to age concern every day in Camden and I help do their window display. My favourite colour is magenta and the biggest word I can write is rhododendron. I know you like to work with people who are different and have good ideas. I can make a handbag out of crushed cola bottle tops and I have my own tailor's dummy, which I can bring with me on the aeroplane.

I have drawn on the envelope to you and I can sew really neatly.

The only thing I would like is that my ferret Flick can live in New York, too. You will never know she is there, Mr Marallino.

My birthday is in June, if you want me to start work then.

Yours sincerely,

Marta G. Ziegler

Fantastic Books
Great Authors

Meet our authors and discover our exciting range of books:

- Gripping Thrillers
- Cosy Mysteries
- Romantic Chick-Lit
- Fascinating Historicals
- Exciting Fantasy
- Young Adult and Children's Adventures

Visit us at:
www.crookedcatpublishing.com

Join us on facebook:
www.facebook.com/crookedcatpublishing

Printed in Great Britain
by Amazon.co.uk, Ltd.,
Marston Gate.